Jenny didn't believe in love at first sight

Then she met Eric Delmont and knew immediately he was the man for her. He felt the same way, she was sure, for he practically proposed on their first date. Then without a word of explanation he disappeared.

Fortunately, Jenny's job as a travel agent kept her busy, taking her to Marrakesh, to Copenhagen, to Madrid. She was shocked when she started running into Eric—often surrounded by beautiful women. More than shocked, for his presence in every city corresponded with major art and jewel thefts....

Was she in love with a thief? And was her love drawing her deeper and deeper into a vortex of violence?

EXPERIENCE THE THRILL OF LOVE...AND DANGER!

MYSTIQUE BOOKS bring you the thrill of suspense and romance in a breathless blend that will leave you eager for more.

MYSTIQUE BOOKS take you into a world where idyllic love is mysteriously threatened. You'll travel to such exotic places as the sunny Caribbean, romantic Paris, the white beaches of Cyprus or the intimidating streets of Istanbul. But wherever you go, romance proves to be a dangerous encounter.

You'll love these exciting, adventure-filled books. Each is an unforgettable reading experience. Four new titles are published every month. Look for them wherever paperback books are sold.

A Touch
of Terror

by CLAUDETTE BERT

MYSTIQUE BOOKS
TORONTO·LONDON·NEW YORK
HAMBURG·AMSTERDAM·STOCKHOLM

Chapter 1

The blue Peugeot rounded the last bend of the mile-long driveway. Like faithful sentinels, ancient stands of oak and ash trees lined the graveled approach, obscuring the view ahead. Suddenly the vegetation cleared and Château des Fleurs burst upon the night in full splendor, its every window ablaze with dancing lights.

Jenny Gordon leaned forward in her seat, pressing her nose close against the glass of the windshield, while her friend negotiated the car around an icy curve.

"What do you see?" Anne asked, her nose wrinkled and her black eyes pushed into a squint as she tried to see past the frost that covered her side of the windshield.

"Snow," answered Jenny.

"Snow?" Anne sighed, giving Jenny a pained expression. "This is the most important moment of my entire life and all you see is . . . snow?"

Jenny laughed. "Okay, I'll look harder."

"Do that, please," ordered her friend primly as she

downshifted into second gear. Slowly they approached the circular drive in front of the huge manor house.

Jenny rubbed at the inside of the window with her glove. "I can see . . . ."

"What?"

"A car."

"So? What kind of a car? All I can see are taillights."

"It's a Rolls-Royce." Jenny looked back at her friend. Anne appeared enraptured by the news.

"Perfect . . . a Rolls." She seemed to savor the information.

For Anne's sake, Jenny strained to make out the scene transpiring in front of the huge double doorway leading into the château. "Oh, Anne . . . you're going to love this. They've got servants dressed in costumes—like footmen. One of them just helped a lady out of the Rolls. There's a man with her, too."

"What are they doing? Can you see?" Anne swiped desperately at her clouded window, trying to see for herself.

"They're freezing," Jenny reported matter-of-factly. "And it looks as if they're hurrying like crazy to get inside where it's warm."

"That's *it*?" Anne looked disappointed.

"Sorry, that's it. What did you want?"

"I don't know," Anne mused. "Something romantic. Something exciting."

"Don't despair, the night's young yet."

Anne shook her head back and forth disbelievingly. "Can you imagine, Jenny; me, plain little Anne Dubois, the hairdresser, being here at a place like this? Do you realize I'm actually going to rub elbows with all those fabulous people? And on Christmas Eve. . . ."

"First of all," Jenny reprimanded good-naturedly, "you're not plain, and you know it. You're just fishing for compliments."

Anne grinned.

"And, second of all, just because some of those people have a lot of money and fancy titles, that doesn't make them any better than us. They're just people, when you get right down to it."

Horrified, Anne widened her dark eyes. "Jenny . . . bite your tongue. Those people aren't just ordinary mortals. When you wear a dress with pearls sewn into the bodice and they're real pearls, well, my dear . . . that *isn't* being an ordinary mortal. When you own a yacht with a swimming pool on board, that's *not* being an ordinary mortal."

Jenny forced herself to remain silent. She'd only spoil Anne's fun if she said what she really thought: that she would much rather be home in Paris with her family; that she was going to be bored silly having to attend a party at which neither she nor Anne belonged; and that Anne, at twenty-two, would be far better off if she thought about marriage to a nice man who'd love her, rather than pursuing her ridiculous dream of catching a rich, titled one. She loved Anne like a sister, but sometimes found her very trying.

She looked across at the woman sitting beside her. Anne's dark eyes sparkled with excitement. Her short brown hair was arranged in soft curls that framed her face becomingly, yet added to the endearing, impish quality that she conveyed to the world.

Perhaps she was wrong to judge Anne's ambitions as being foolish. After all, if she were perfectly honest, her own hopes for the future would sound every bit as fantastic to someone who didn't share her view.

Hadn't she put aside the quite sensible plan of studying law in college for the illusory dream of becoming an artist? She had returned to the United States, where she had been born, to get her degree in art at the University of California. After graduating, it was only natural she should continue her studies at the Sorbonne, for not only did her family live in Paris, but the city, with its breathtaking beauty, was a living treasure for any aspiring artist.

At present she spent her days pleasantly, working in a travel agency. But her evenings were spent rapturously, studying painting and sculpting, as she pursued her own tentative dream. No—she had no right to find fault with Anne's ambitions.

The Peugeot lurched to a stop, lightly bumping into the back end of the Rolls-Royce, still parked in front of the château. Anne gave a groan of psychic pain and grasped her steering wheel tightly with both hands.

The driver of the Rolls opened his door and walked slowly to the back of the long silver car. Apparently satisfied that his owner's vehicle was still intact, he tipped his hat and ambled back to his warm seat, the incident forgotten.

"Phew," Jenny whispered. "We almost made quite an entrance."

"I could just die. Of all the mortifying things to happen; do you think anyone saw?" Anne moaned, looking around.

"Just him," said Jenny, as Anne's door was swept open by a smiling, costumed footman.

Ignoring the wide grin of amusement, Anne struggled to maintain her dignity as she was helped from the car. Jenny let herself out and waited for her friend to come around to her side.

Before them stood the imposing structure of Château des Fleurs. Beyond the thick stone walls, sounds of laughter could be heard over strains of Christmas music played by a live orchestra.

"Oh," Anne breathed, grabbing hold of Jenny's arm as she tried to keep her balance on the slick pavement beneath their feet. "Have you ever seen anything so absolutely impressive?"

Jenny was speechless with awe. She stared up at the hundreds of mullioned windows, the graceful colonnades, the turrets covered in snow, looking like mountain peaks as they extended toward the black sky. It seemed incredible that this was someone's home rather than a museum.

Inside, the party was in full swing. A team of butlers, resplendent in old-fashioned liveried outfits, relieved arriving guests of their wraps—mostly furs, Jenny was quickly informed by Anne, as if her friend were worried she had failed to note the phenomenon herself.

They found themselves within a huge hall, the focal point being a towering Christmas tree decorated with hundreds of colored bulbs and electric lights. Guests in formal attire wandered through the main hall in small groups, disappearing into rooms on either side as they joined other friends.

"Well?" asked Jenny, craning her neck to get a better view of a well-known actress. "Which roomful of dignitaries shall we dazzle first?"

"That one," Anne said, and pointed discreetly in the direction of a double door, its face elaborately carved in the likeness of flower garlands.

"Mmm," Jenny nodded knowingly, "and I see why."

Just outside the room, a tall, blond and decidedly

elegant man stood talking with another man, shorter and slightly balding.

"What do you think?" Anne whispered, leaning slightly toward Jenny as they walked. "Think he's rich?"

"I'm not sure about his financial status, but he's not bad-looking," Jenny whispered back and laughed.

Anne stopped suddenly, clutching at Jenny's arm.

"That man . . . the other one; not the Greek god. That's the marquis! The unmarried, unattached, single, marriagable marquis who owns all of this," Anne said reverently, indicating the room with a sweep of her large brown eyes. "Come on, Jen; I think I'm in love."

Anne led Jenny through the main hall, a room done completely in marble, with marble pillars spaced every twenty feet, and black and white marble squares that formed geometric patterns on the floor.

Walking gingerly across the highly waxed stone, they passed the two men talking by the door and entered what they found to be the drawing room.

"Well . . . did he notice me?" Anne asked immediately. "I was trying to be aloof, so I couldn't look."

"Sorry—he was having a chat with the Greek god; didn't even know we were there, I'm afraid."

"Oh, bother! Well, what did he say?"

"My, my, aren't you inquisitive," Jenny chided with a light laugh. "Really, though," she said, suddenly serious, "it was strange. Unless I'm mistaken, the marquis said to be careful, and he said something about there being danger, too."

"Oh, is that all?" Anne was obviously disappointed. "Well, then, I'm going back out there. I didn't go through all the trouble to get an invitation to this bash from my hoity-toity patron, just to stand around and munch hors d'oeuvres."

With that she swept from the room, her long blue dress swishing regally behind her, leaving Jenny to survey the drawing room at her leisure. For the time being, it appeared that she was to be on her own while Anne laid a trap for the unsuspecting marquis.

The room, she discovered, was decidedly sumptuous, its decor formal. Vivid blue and gold Lyon silk had been used for the draperies and also for the upholstered Louis XVI chairs and sofas. As if in competition with their surroundings, the guests had also dressed in elaborately formal attire.

Jenny found her attention drawn to a middle-aged woman with silver hair worn in an upsweep. Her gown was white, with panels of white sequins sewn over the skirt, and while a magnificent dress, it was only a background for the ruby-and-diamond necklace that glistened majestically around her neck.

Jenny's absorption was so intense that she was surprised at the presence of a tall man who had moved close to her side. It was the "Greek god" who had been talking to the marquis.

Without being obvious she studied his profile, realizing that his attention was also riveted on the stunning woman in white, with the dazzling necklace at her throat.

As if he sensed her eyes on him, the man turned abruptly to face her directly. Jenny blushed and looked away, embarrassed that her interest in him was so obvious.

Rather than look away, he continued his appraisal of her, and from the corner of her eye, Jenny was well aware of the obvious appreciation reflected in his glance.

Oddly, she didn't find his look insolent; rather, it seemed one of professional observation. She herself adopted a similar attitude when she critically appraised a fine piece of artwork. The idea that she was being judged in such a manner seemed absurdly amusing, and in spite of herself, she laughed.

As if he understood, the tall stranger returned a faint smile. For a moment Jenny thought he would speak; but she was wrong. His attention shifted from her back to the woman in white.

Pausing now and then, the woman moved through the room, exchanging pleasantries with other guests. It was clear she was headed for the door leading from the room into the great hall.

The man next to Jenny tensed. She saw him glance quickly at his watch, then lower his arm, appearing visibly relieved.

It was an awkward situation. Many of the guests had already moved from the room and entered the expansive hall, gathering around the massive tree to listen to the carolers. Neither she nor the attractive man next to her had actually moved, yet the distance between them seemed to have closed.

She was very much aware of his cologne, of him. The surrounding room, with all its furniture and art treasures, seemed to have melted away, and all that existed in her private universe were herself and the man standing beside her.

To walk away now, when they were so close, would appear rude. Yet if she stayed . . . if he spoke to her . . . the magic she now felt would most certainly be shattered.

It was clear they were from different worlds. The cut of his dark blue velvet dinner jacket was expensive, its fine stitching all but invisible to the eye. The shirt he wore was elaborate, but on him, served to accentuate his masculinity. The total effect reflected the well-bred air associated with the elite, a status that precluded the petty rules governing the lives of men born to lesser privilege.

She knew they would have nothing in common; there would be nothing for them to speak of and she'd only embarrass herself with her comparative lack of sophistication. If Anne didn't know when she was out of her league, at least she did.

She took a step forward to leave.

"If you are planning on joining your friend, she's busy."

Jenny turned to the man next to her. "I beg your pardon? My friend? But how could you know—"

"I saw you both come into the room earlier," he explained. His deep blue eyes bore only the slightest hint of amusement. Other than that spark, his manner was one of disinterest, coupled with a certain world-weariness. "I believe," he continued, "that she is presently being entertained by a boring, but very rich viscount."

Jenny had begun to feel like a specimen under glass. How much else had the man noticed about her, she wondered. But before she could respond to his last statement, he spoke again.

"Would you care to hear the carolers?"

"I—"

"Neither would I," he finished for her. "I'd find a stroll with you much more to my liking."

There was no opportunity to protest. Having made his pronouncement, it was—for him—a decision made. Jenny automatically took his proferred arm.

He led her into the hall, smoothly navigating their passage through the crowd of drinking and laughing guests, and although she was close, touching against his arm and able to feel the strength of his shoulder against her as she walked beside him, she had the unmistakable impression that his mind was elsewhere. Certainly it was not on her, of that she was sure.

Stealing a surreptitious glance, she saw him scan the crowded hall. Plainly he was looking for someone.

Another woman, of course. It was obvious. He was an attractive man—an incredibly attractive man, she corrected herself—at a party filled with the cream of society, and some very, very beautiful women.

Across the room Jenny noticed the woman with the white dress and ruby-and-diamond necklace. She had just turned away the carolers and was walking up the winding marble staircase.

Her escort seemed to notice, too. He spoke immediately. "Have you seen the library on the second floor?"

"No . . . no, I haven't. But my friend says it's spectacular. She's read about it—I mean heard about it," Jenny qualified, realizing Anne would look rather foolish is he knew she pored over the gossip columns as if the state of the world hung on the latest party's success.

"Your friend . . . yes," he said absently, his mind evidently elsewhere as he led her to the stairs.

Jenny walked faster, keeping match with his stride.

The woman in white had almost reached the top landing. From their position lower on the stairs, Jenny saw her turn and move toward the right.

A moment later they, too, had reached the top landing. Jenny was steered quickly toward the right, just as the woman disappeared through a doorway. The door shut silently behind her.

Jenny's partner seemed strangely concerned. His mouth

was drawn into a stern line and his eyes, which had been clear and vital a moment before, were now cold and blue gray, like steel.

"Looks like you've lost her," Jenny said, aware that she had been forgotton.

"What?" From his superior height he looked down upon her, making her feel much smaller than her five and a half feet.

"I assume we were trying to catch the mysterious lady in white?" Jenny quipped. "But, alas . . . it looks as if she escaped. So, why didn't we follow? What's in the room, anyway?"

"That particular door leads to a most luxurious powder room, or so I've been told. Exclusive to ladies," he added dryly. "Now, since I believe that piece of information answers your questions, shall we visit the library?"

Jenny colored, feeling foolish to have made so much out of so little. He led her past the ladies' powder room and down a wide hallway with branches of other, more narrow, hallways shooting off it, like small branches from a tree's main trunk.

A large, carved oak door opened into a cavernous room lined floor to ceiling with bookshelves containing leatherbound volumes of world classics as well as recent editions of best-sellers. Scattered throughout the room were comfortable leather chairs and a pair of matching tufted, redleather sofas, which faced each other in front of a crackling fire.

Jenny stared in wonderment at her surroundings, while her companion poured snifters of brandy from a crystal decanter and warmed them over a flame on a silver stand.

When he walked over to her, carrying both glasses, she noticed a change in his attitude. He was more relaxed, as if being away from the crowded party had allowed him to be at ease.

"You're a very mysterious young woman yourself," he said, handing her the warmed glass of liquid.

"Me? Mysterious?" Jenny thought of her appearance and the impression she presumed she was making. She had worn her long green dress, with the scooped neckline and tight fitted sleeves. She had assumed she looked festive, not mysterious.

"I don't even know your name," he said in a low, intimate voice. "And I asked someone—the moment I saw you."

Jenny's heart quickened. The most attractive man she had ever met was paying her a compliment. She could hardly believe her ears—or her luck.

"Then I'm at precisely the same disadvantage," she managed to say. "For I've been following around a strange man, whose name I don't know, either."

"Eric Delmont," he said, his eyes crinkling softly at the corners. The coldness was gone, replaced by the warmth of a summer's day, eyes the color of bluebells, amused, honest . . . and compelling, Jenny admitted to herself.

"And I'm Jenny Gordon," she replied, realizing that although his French was fluent, like her own, his nationality was obviously English, judging by the slightest accent.

"You're a beautiful woman, Jenny Gordon," he said quite seriously. "But then I suppose you know that already. In fact, you're the most beautiful woman here tonight."

He had spoken so plainly, with such simplicity that Jenny was barely aware that the look in his eyes said more. They had changed again, with mercurial speed, and now burned into her, as if reaching for her very soul.

Something—an emotion akin to fear—made her fight

against the moment. "I don't really belong here," she blurted. "Not here at the château; not with all these people."

The man named Eric Delmont gave her a questioning look.

"What I mean is," she continued, turning to the fire, "my friend, whom I love dearly, but who has some peculiar ideas at times, arranged to get invitations for us tonight. She persuaded me to come."

"Against your better judgment?"

"Yes, exactly." She smiled, feeling better now that she had confessed her social pretensions.

"Then where do you belong, Jenny Gordon? Tell me," he said, motioning to the sofa. "I want to know everything about you."

Much to her surprise, Jenny spoke for the next hour, encouraged at every step by a warm smile, an understanding nod, a comment of interest and compassion. She was not in the habit of divulging her life history to complete strangers, but unaccountably, she felt as if she'd known Eric Delmont for years. She told him of her childhood, of how her mother had died when she was only three months old, and of how she had been educated in American private schools, receiving the best of tuition, but little warmth or love.

Her father, she told him, had worked for a multinational engineering firm. His work had taken him to foreign countries, where he supervised the building of bridges and high-rise structures.

Rarely did she see him, and when they did meet, the relationship had been strained. In reality, they had been no more than strangers, with paths that crossed at infrequent intervals.

When she was thirteen her father had remarried. His

new wife was a Frenchwoman and Jenny moved to France to live. It was then her life had changed. Her stepmother showered her with affection, smothering her with long-desired attention and approval. She encouraged Jenny's interest in art, providing her with paper, paints, clay—everything to promote her talents.

Then, her stepbrothers were born—first Allan, then Michael, her favorite. So for years she had had no family, and then she had so much—so much love and so many happy, tender moments.

Strangely, it was as if her father had known that he must make amends for his life before it was too late. But too late came too soon. Shortly after Michael was born, her father was killed in a car accident in Germany.

Jenny paused in her story, unable to go on. Lost in the world of her past, her green eyes had filled with tears. She looked up, surprised to find that Eric Delmont's face mirrored the pain she felt in her heart.

He reached for her hand, pulling her gently to him and encircled her within his arms. "Jenny," he said softly, his voice intense with emotion, "where have you been? I've looked for you for so long."

Then, pushing her away from him, he held her at arm's length, searching her face for an answer to some unvoiced question.

"This is crazy," Jenny said. "I know what I feel, and it's wonderful. But it's also impossible. We hardly know each other."

Eric was quiet for a moment. His face was serious when he spoke. "Jenny, I don't want tonight to end . . . I don't want you and me to end. This is strange for me, too, believe me. In fact, it's incredible, and it's fast. But Jenny . . . I know that it's real."

"I know, too," she whispered.

"I want to see you tomorrow."

"Tomorrow's Christmas."

"Spend it with me?" Eric asked, his eyes insisting.

"Eric, I can't. My family is counting on me to be with them. Christmas is so special to Allan and Michael. And to my stepmother, too. If I weren't there, it would spoil it for them."

"All right." He touched her face with his hand. "I understand. I don't want to make anything difficult for you. I'll let you have Boxing Day with your family too. But the day after that I'm claiming you all to myself. I'll pick you up and we'll spend the whole day together."

Jenny's face fell. "Eric, I can't then, either. I have to work."

"Work?"

It was as if he hadn't the foggiest notion of what the word meant.

"Don't you . . . work?" she asked, suddenly curious as to what he did for a living, and at the same time knowing it would make no difference to her whatsoever.

"I do work, yes. . . ." He paused for barely an instant then said, "I'll pick you up after work." With a shake of his head he amended, "No, could you meet me? I've got an appointment near the Chez Cary. We can dine there."

Jenny knew of the restaurant, reputedly one of the finest in all of Paris. If you weren't rich—very rich—it would be foolhardly even to sniff the expensive air inside.

Eric was apparently lost in thought, making arrangements in his mind. "We'll meet at six o'clock."

Jenny smiled. He had already made the plans and accepted for her. But, of course, she would do what he wanted; after all, she was in love.

Eric leaned closer, and she felt his hand tremble as he gently lifted her chin. Closing her eyes, she shuddered as their lips touched.

Almost simultaneously, the door to the library burst open with a sudden bang.

"Oh! Pardon!" exclaimed a jubilant male voice.

Jenny and Eric broke apart. A portly man dressed in a black tuxedo stood in the doorway. He grinned from ear to ear, obviously pleased with the scene he had interrupted.

Jenny suppressed a giggle. Standing, she said, "I think I'll see for myself just how luxurious the powder room really is."

Eric escorted her to the same door through which the woman in white had passed earlier. Quicky she freshened her makeup and ran a comb through her shoulder-length blond hair. When she returned to the hall, she was certain she hadn't been gone longer than five minutes. But Eric was gone.

For a moment her heart sank, frightened that their encounter in the library had been entirely the work of her imagination. But she could still smell the expensive scent he wore. He *had* been with her . . . and he always would be, she vowed.

But there was no further time to dwell on her future with Eric. The present was very much upon the Château des Fleurs.

A shriek, high-pitched and feminine, sounded from below in the central hall. Jenny heard the excited voices of other guests meld in confused comments.

"Stop him! Thief!" boomed a man's voice, as Jenny leaned over the banister to witness the scene below.

Turning, she looked both ways down the hall, thinking that Eric might have returned, but there was no one around. The hall was empty. Dejected, she made her way down the long staircase.

The woman in white stood sobbing in the center of a concerned crowd of other guests. Her long, tapered fingers clutched at her neck. "My jewels . . . my jewels . . ." she repeated over and over in a litany of anguish.

"My dear, don't fret; they'll get the thief. I know it," a matronly woman comforted, while holding her hand protectively against her own strand of pearls.

The woman in white continued to relive the event for her audience. "I was in the drawing room," she said, "resting for a moment on one of the sofas. Suddenly, I felt a jolt at my neck and before I could turn around—before I even knew what had happened—it was gone. My beautiful necklace had been stolen!" she wailed.

While the woman continued, Jenny scanned the crowd for Eric. He was not among the concerned throng babbling their mystification, expelling their rage, unanimously voicing their objections to the daring heist.

Someone touched her elbow. Smiling, Jenny spun around. "Eric—" The name died on her lips, as did the smile on her face. It was only Anne.

"Isn't it juicy?" Anne squealed, obviously delighted to be present at the crime of the year.

"Juicy?" Jenny stared at her friend, not following her meaning.

"Yes . . . someone saw the thief leave. He's supposed to be young. And handsome!" Anne waited for Jenny's reaction.

"Oh, I see." She really wasn't interested. Her mind was on Eric's disappearance.

"That woman, the one over there—" Anne pointed to an attractive younger woman in a red dress "—she said she saw a man race across the lawn, I mean snow," she corrected, and paused to give Jenny the chance she needed to digest the piece of gossip. "Oh, and this is the best part. He was tall and blond. Dressed formally." Her eyes widened with excitement. "Don't you see what that means?"

Thinking of someone else tall and blond, Jenny made no reply.

Exasperated, Anne threw her hands in the air and explained slowly, as if to a backward child, "Jen—it means that the thief was most likely right here with us this evening!" Her delight seemed complete.

"Anne, I'm feeling a bit tired. It's an hour's ride back home to Paris. Maybe we should go."

"Go?" Anne's face crumbled. "Jen, this is excitement; firsthand. It's bound to be in the papers tomorrow, and for once in my entire life, I'm actually here where it's all happening. I don't just have to read about it—I *am* it!"

"Sorry," Jenny said softly, "I really don't feel well." She wasn't just making an excuse. She had gone from the heights of sublime joy to a shaky feeling of insecurity aggravated by doubt. Where was Eric? Where had he gone? And . . . why had he gone? That was the question that plagued her the most.

"All right. We'll go," Anne relented morosely. "but, just imagine . . . you could have been standing right next to the thief and not have even known it."

"No!" Jenny shot back. "I would have known it; I'm sure I would."

Chapter 2

Christmas Day had passed as if it had been a dream.

Jenny had laughed, she had exclaimed over the presents she had received from Allan and Michael, she had helped serve the fabulous dinner her stepmother had prepared, but her heart and mind had been elsewhere.

The image of Eric Delmont occupied her every waking thought. She could see him perfectly; tall—at least six two—the incredible deep blue eyes; sandy-blond hair that waved slightly; the strong, square set of his jaw; and a nose that was straight and perfect. Anne had called him a Greek god. The description was remarkably apt.

Likewise Boxing Day passed . . . somehow. Now it was Tuesday, and time to go back to work. But today was special. Today, at six o'clock, she would be with Eric again.

It was half-past six and she had to be at work by nine-o'clock. She had purposely set her alarm for an hour earlier than usual, so she'd have extra time to dress. Tonight she had to look beautiful.

She was used to receiving her share of compliments.
Even when she was a child, people had stared at her. As a
teenager, she had been overwhelmed by the attention she
had received from teenage boys, and now her stepmother
proudly proclaimed that she had blossomed into a true
beauty.

This morning, as she gazed at her reflection in the mirror, she wanted to believe that this was true. She wanted to
be beautiful for Eric!

Eyes the color of the sea on a calm day stared back at her
from across her vanity table. She applied a light touch of
blue eye shadow to her upper lids, and as if by magic, the
shade of her eyes seemed to change and grow darker, more
vivid. Quickly she applied a hint of blusher to her high
cheekbones. Fair and nearly flawless, her complexion
never required the use of foundation makeup. Her lashes
were dark and thick, emphasizing the dramatic green of
her eyes.

Her hair was shoulder-length and thick and honey
blond. She thought of the elegant women she had seen the
night at the château and decided to wear it up in a graceful
twist, rather than loose over her shoulders.

Since she would be meeting Eric in the evening, she'd
need to wear something more formal than usual to work.
A quick survey of her wardrobe made her heart sink; she
had only one suitable dress. Well, at least that made the
selection easy. The dress of white wool had long sleeves, a
straight skirt, and a square neckline above a becomingly
fitted bodice.

The effect, as she stood back looking at herself in the
mirror, was refined and understated. But it needed
something. Color. She rushed to her jewelry chest, opened
it, and searched for the strand of jade and gold beads that

her father had brought from the Orient before he had died.

Finding it, she held it between her fingers for a moment, remembering the day she had received it. Then another, unbidden, thought crossed her mind, and it wasn't a pleasant one.

She recalled the party at the château, seeing once again the stricken face of the woman in white and hearing her voice lament the theft of her precious stones. A tall, blond young man had been seen leaving the château. Eric was tall, blond and young. And Eric had mysteriously disappeared. . . .

Quickly Jenny shut out the unwelcome thought. She was being ridiculous. How could she even entertain the notion that Eric could have anything to do with the stolen necklace? She was a typical artist blessed with an overactive imagination, and in this case it needed to be held in check.

There was a logical explanation for Eric's disappearance, she was sure, and tonight at six-o'clock at the Chez Cary, he would tell her what it was.

MONICA WAS ALREADY TYPING invoices when Jenny entered the travel agency at nine o'clock.

"Nice of you to drop in," Monica said sourly, looking up from the typewriter.

Surprised at her co-worker's sarcastic tone, Jenny looked at her sharply for a moment, then decided to ignore the cut. "Did you have a nice Christmas?" she asked instead.

"Rotten."

"Oh . . . sorry."

Jenny slid into her desk chair after hanging up her coat. Nothing could ruin the mood she was in. "My Christmas was lovely," she offered, hoping to change the atmosphere. It was a mistake. She saw—or rather heard—how wrong she had been almost immediately.

"Isn't that just ducky? Everything is always so lovely for you." Monica glared at Jenny from across her desk.

This time, Jenny was stunned at the young woman's outburst. Monica was seldom the most friendly and diplomatic of persons, but this was a little vitriolic even for her. "That really isn't true, you know," she murmured after a moment.

"Come on, Jenny," protested Monica. "You've got a family that pampers you, you've been to the best schools, and with your face and figure, you don't even have to know how to talk."

Jenny wasn't sure whether she had just been handed an insult or a compliment. "Listen," she said, getting up and walking to Monica's desk. "Things haven't been quite as easy for me as it seems. I just don't believe in dwelling on the negative all the time."

"I know," sighed the young woman, "and I'm sorry. didn't really mean to take my anger out on you. It's just that lately my whole life seems to be negative."

"What do you want out of life?" Jenny asked gently, for she felt sorry for the dark-haired girl with the sad brown eyes.

Monica thought for a moment. "Really want to know?"

"Yes."

"I'd like to find a terrific man. I'd like to fall in love—or rather, I'd like him to fall in love with me. For once. Instead of it always being the other way around."

"Yes . . . I know what you mean," said Jenny softly, thinking of Eric.

"And I'd like to get married and live happily ever after," concluded Monica.

"It could happen," Jenny said, trying to put a cheery note in her voice.

"Yeah . . . sure," mumbled her co-worker. "And pigs could fly." She reached for another piece of paper to put in her typewriter. "But you know the worst part about it? Sometimes, when I look around when I'm out at lunch or shopping, I see all these couples together, laughing and holding hands . . . and I almost hate them. It just doesn't seem fair."

The telephone on Jenny's desk rang and she left Monica to her self-pity.

The rest of the day passed slowly. Time seemed frozen, with the magic hour of six o'clock an eternity away as Jenny booked clients on excursions to exotic lands.

When she finally left the office for the day, it was dark and cold outside.

She was fifteen minutes late meeting Eric because of congested traffic. By the time the taxi stopped in front of the Chez Cary Jenny's heart was beating wildly. What if Eric had left the restaurant, thinking she wasn't coming? The thought filled her with panic, and she quickly paid the driver, leaving him an extravagant tip rather than wait for her change.

A doorman smiled stiffly to her as she entered the restaurant. Unlike newer restaurants, the Chez Cary had a subdued, well-worn interior decor. It had made its name among the world's finest restaurants several generations before, and now its ambience was one of moneyed tradition rather than superficial flash.

Her worst fears were never realized; Eric waited in the foyer.

"Jenny," he said, taking hold of her hand and squeezing it within his own, as if fearful she might evaporate if he didn't hang onto her. "For a few moments—terrible moments—I thought you might not come."

"I was afraid you wouldn't wait."

"For you? I'd have waited here all night." His smile was dazzling as he looked into her eyes.

They were led immediately to their table, where with great ceremony a haughty waiter clucked with approval over their choices for dinner.

At Eric's suggestion Jenny was beginning the meal with a *terrine de foie gras de Strasbourg*, served with a fine champagne retrieved from the wine cellar. Accompanied by much pomp, the owner himself insisted on opening the bottle, exclaiming in superlatives on its excellence and complimenting Eric on his choice.

Clearly Eric had made an impression on the staff, but his own attention was trained exclusively on Jenny.

"Do you realize," he said in a serious tone, "if you hadn't come this evening, I'd have had no way of ever finding you?"

Jenny paled at the very thought. "You're absolutely right." Without wasting another moment, she reached into her purse and pulled out a pen and paper. "Here," she said, "you can reach me at the travel agency. Sorry, but we haven't been flush enough to have a phone at home, not since dad died."

Eric glanced at the number on the paper and opened his jacket to produce a minuscule telephone book covered in alligator skin. In a minute he had written her number in the book. "That way I'll be sure to have it with me," he explained.

As he reached within his jacket to return the directory, something dislodged itself from an interior pocket and fell onto the table. It was a book of matches; but not just any book of matches, Jenny noted.

"May I?" she asked, gesturing to them. Picking them up, she turned the small package over in her hand, noticing how slim it was. Its cover was of a royal purple felt, but to the touch it was very much like velveteen.

"It's beautiful," she said, running her finger over the engraved gold scrollwork covering it face.

"Keep them, if you like. I don't smoke. I only carry them with me for my friends who run out of matches."

Jenny dropped them in her purse, preferring to spend the time looking at Eric, for at the moment she felt that she would never tire of the sight of his handsome face, which looked especially attractive in the flickering candlelight.

While they talked, she was vaguely aware that the restaurant had become more crowded. Occasionally people would pass their table and she would pause in her conversation to fleetingly admire a woman's gown, or the dignity of an older man who seemed to know everyone. This was a part of life she had never experienced. She had never considered herself a country bumpkin exactly, having traveled throughout Europe and the United States; but these people moved in a rarefied atmosphere beyond anything in her experience.

There was a slight murmur in the restaurant, and Jenny turned her head to see a young woman enter.

Eric turned, also, following Jenny's gaze. He gave a slight start, which did not go unnoticed by Jenny. Certainly the woman who had just entered the room was really beautiful, but she couldn't help wondering if perhaps Eric knew her.

The woman in question was slowly walking in their direction. Accompanied by an attractive man of perhaps forty, she herself could not have been more than twenty-five years old.

Her hair was a soft shade of red, worn long and full, so

that it billowed around her in a cloud as she walked. Her eyes were deep brown, round and surprisingly innocent in comparison to her full and sensuous mouth. She looked like an expensive doll; a hand-crafted work of art glorifying the beauty of womanhood.

She had almost passed their table when she stopped suddenly, as if she'd just noticed them.

"Why, Eric," she said, her wide smile of greeting displaying a set of even teeth. "Darlin', I had absolutely no idea that ya'll were going to be here tonight." Her glance fell lightly on Jenny.

Jenny tried to smile, knowing that what she produced was more closely akin to a crooked grimace.

Eric rose from his chair. "Candy McManus . . . Jennifer Gordon."

"How do you do, Miss Gordon?" Candy drawled.

"Miss McManus. . . ." Jenny returned stiffly, hoping her insecurity didn't show.

"Oh, Eric, darlin', darn but I have to run along now. I'm with the most tiresome man," she informed them, as her companion talked to someone at a nearby table. "Daddy insisted I let him take me to dinner," she added quietly, her lowered voice losing none of its suggestively breathless quality.

"We understand; truly. . . ." Eric commented graciously.

"Darlin', you know I'd much rather have spent the evening with someone fun. Like you."

Eric had the grace to appear mildly uncomfortable. He shot Jenny a quick glance, to which she responded with an icy stare. It seemed, however, that Candy McManus was reluctant to depart.

"Now, don't you forget tomorrow night," she cooed, blowing him a kiss as she wafted off to join her date.

Eric smiled sheepishly. "I know what you're thinking," he began.

"Really?" Jenny said, feigning indifference as she lifted her glass of champagne to her lips. She hoped her hand didn't shake.

"Candy's an old friend of the family's. Or, rather, her family is an old friend of my family's."

"How terribly nice." How terrible convenient, was more likely, thought Jenny as she met Eric's guileless blue eyes.

"Candy's from Texas," he offered.

"I gathered that, from the moment she opened her little ol' mouth," replied Jenny, mimicking the young woman's drawl. Her imitation was flawless, as she had shared a room in college with a girl from Dallas.

For a moment Eric just looked at her. He had leaned back into his chair and looked comfortably cool and detached. "I'm flattered," he said at last. "It appears that you are jealous of my relationship—such as it is—with Miss McManus."

"Of course not," Jenny replied, the beginnings of a smile touching her lips. "Why on earth would I be jealous of her? I mean, she's certainly very beautiful, and judging by the jewelry she wore, very rich, too. Whatever could you possibly see in someone like her?"

There was a moment of silence, then both she and Eric burst out laughing at the same instant. The whole situation suddenly seemed utterly ridiculous. She had met Eric just two days ago, and already she was being possessive.

"Don't change, Jenny. I want you to care; I want you to want me for yourself," Eric said, when finally they stopped laughing. "And just to prove it . . . I've got something for you."

As he spoke, he reached into his jacket pocket and drew

out a small black velvet box. In it was an enormous green stone in a simple silver setting, attached to a delicate, intricately woven, silver chain.

Jenny was stunned. "It's . . . it's magnificent," she stammered breathlessly, her eyes never leaving the stone.

"Yes, the emerald's been in my family for two centuries. I want you to have it."

"Eric, I couldn't," she gasped, looking up at him in disbelief. Her green eyes, the same color as the pendant, were filled with tears. "It's the most beautiful piece of jewelry I've ever seen, and I'm so touched . . . but no."

"Take it," he said calmly. "Put it on. And don't ever take it off. Not until I replace it with something else," he said.

"But it's an heirloom," she objected. "You just said that it's been in your family for two hundred years."

"Exactly, and that's why I want you to have it. I plan to see that it remains in the family."

Jenny's heart almost stopped. Did he mean what she thought he meant? No; she must be misinterpreting his words. It was a beautiful piece of jewelry—and obviously valuable. But perhaps his family was so wealthy he could afford to part with a stone such as this.

Her head was spinning; nothing made sense. She was afraid to keep the stone, but just as afraid not to accept it. He seemed so adamant. Very well, she decided. She'd take the stone, and on another occasion when the atmosphere was less charged, she'd graciously return it to him.

With trembling fingers she removed her own necklace and fastened the clasp of Eric's around her neck. Suddenly a cloud passed over her, marring the happiness of the moment. The cold touch of the stone against her throat brought back the image of a woman in white wearing a ruby-and-diamond necklace.

"Jenny? Is something wrong?" Eric asked, leaning over the table with a concerned look on his face. "You aren't sick, are you?"

"No, I'm fine," she lied. In fact, she wasn't fine at all. She wanted to ask him about the night at the party. She knew it was stupid—no, wrong—even to think that he might know something about the theft. Yet it had bothered her all of yesterday and again today that he hadn't said goodbye to her and had mysteriously disappeared at the same time the necklace had been reported stolen. Nor had he said anything so far this evening to explain his strange behavior.

"Something's bothering you and I want you to tell me what it is," said Eric authoritatively. "It's not Candy, is it?"

Jenny smiled briefly and shook her head. What could she say? She certainly couldn't ask him about the other night—it would be the worst kind of insult. But perhaps she could lead on to the topic another way. . . .

"Eric," she said, "I've told you so much about myself, but you've barely told me anything about your own life."

She watched his reaction. His blue eyes were steady, his face almost expressionless. Too expressionless, she considered. It was as if he were thinking, gathering his thoughts before he spoke, and the slight pause before he answered made her feel uncomfortable.

"Obviously, I was mistaken; I thought we had shared a great deal of information," he said at last. "We know we both enjoy the same things: sports, travel, art. Each other. . . ."

"Yes, it's just that—"

"Ah! You want to know what I do for a living," he finished for her.

How terrible he made it sound. She must appear like

Anne—a veritable golddigger. Had she imagined the reproach behind his words?

"Would it make a difference to you, Jenny?" he asked solemnly.

"Eric, no! Of course not," she rushed. "You must know that. It wouldn't matter to me what you did. Please, believe me."

There was that same gleam of detached amusement in his eyes.

"I might be a carpenter," he remarked casually.

"That's an honorable trade. But then really, coming here tonight must have wiped out a whole month of your wages," she replied, knowing she was being teased.

"On the other hand, I might be a racing-car driver."

"And that's a dangerous profession. No, I wouldn't be keen on that; not at all."

"Good. Because I'm not." He hesitated for a moment, his attention apparently caught by something across the room. Jenny followed his gaze and turned to see a man a woman rising from their table. They were an older couple, distinguished-looking and very well-to-do, judging by the fur stole the woman wore across her shoulders.

As she got to her feet, she let her stole slip lower on her back. A sparkle flashed near her neck and Jenny realized she was wearing a diamond necklace that had just picked up the light of a nearby chandelier.

The man had taken the woman's arm and was leading her through the room toward the door to the outside foyer when Eric moved suddenly, pushing his chair away from the table. Jenny gave him a questioning look.

"You'll excuse me?" He seemed in a hurry—preoccupied. "I have to make a telephone call. I'd almost forgotten. . . ." His voice trailed off.

"Yes . . . yes, of course," she said at once.

He was gone from the table within a second. Jenny watched him move through the room, his long strides carrying him rapidly toward the foyer. Several diners turned their heads in his direction. There was no doubt he was a striking figure, and Jenny was proud that he commanded the respect and admiration she saw reflected in curious eyes around the room.

The minutes passed slowly. According to her watch Eric had been gone for ten minutes. Had she offended him after all, she wondered. Perhaps he had used the telephone call as an excuse to leave her.

Finally she could stand the waiting and doubt no longer. Rising from her seat, she was about to go in search of him when she heard a commotion coming from the entrance to the restaurant.

Several of the waiters had gathered together, their heads bent as they whispered confidentially among themselves.

The elderly gentleman who had just left the dining room with the woman in the fur stole rushed back into the room with the owner of the restaurant at his side.

"No, no!" the older man insisted. "I tell you she was wearing the diamonds when she left this room. I'm sure of it!"

Several members of the staff combed the area by the table, checking every inch of the path the couple had taken when they walked from the room.

Jenny blanched. Still standing by her chair, she gripped its back tightly, looking almost furtively around the room. Everyone in the restaurant was exclaiming as they checked their own jewelry, and at the same time they cast suspicious stares at fellow diners.

Where was Eric? Why hadn't he returned? Almost

stumbling as she rushed from the room, Jenny tripped up the three steps that led from the main room up into the foyer.

"Excuse me . . . please," she said to a passing waiter. "The telephone? Where may I find it?"

"Over there," he said, pointing down a narrow hall.

Her heart sank when she reached it. There was no one there. Not a soul.

At a loss, she returned to the entrance and there, by the cashier, stood Eric. He had just handed the man at the register a handful of bills, along with what appeared to be the check for their meal.

Jenny crossed to him, almost at a run. But Eric was in an even greater hurry. With lightning speed he walked to the front door and pushed it open; then, for just an instant, he whirled around and looked into the restaurant.

Jenny's eyes locked with his. It was a moment suspended in time. Then he was gone.

The door shut behind him, leaving her alone for the second time in three days; leaving her alone with no explanation.

No, she decided. This time she'd find him. She'd catch up with the disappearing Eric Delmont and find out exactly what his game was.

Grabbing her coat from the cloakroom attendant, she threw open the door to the restaurant. But it was too late. At the curb stood a taxi, and in it was Eric Delmont, leaning over the front seat and gesticulating ahead.

With a roar and a terrifying squeal of tires on pavement, the cab tore off into the night.

Chapter 3

Monica was slumped over her desk, working on some papers when Jenny arrived at work on Wednesday morning.

"You're late," Monica said, looking up with a gloomy expression.

"Sorry," replied Jenny, as she hung up her coat and scarf. Outside it was snowing lightly, and she brushed away some random white flakes from her hair. "It's the first time, anyway."

Monica, back at work again, made no comment.

"Any messages?" queried Jenny.

"On your desk."

Jenny had asked the question casually, but her heart leaped as she picked up the stack of telephone calls that had come in for her. *Please, please, let Eric have called.* She bit her lip in disappointment.

All the messages were from clients—nice people, but none of them Eric.

Monica had raised her head, and was watching her closely.

"What's the matter?" she asked.

"Nothing."

"Sure there is. I know that expression. I ought to—I wear it often enough myself. It's a man, huh?"

"What?" Jenny was thinking about the previous evening. She was sure that Eric would have called to explain.

"You've got trouble with a man. Isn't that right?"

"No one else called me, did they, Monica?"

The young woman seemed to think for a moment. "No. Who were you expecting? Prince Charles?"

"Listen, Monica," Jenny said, "there's someone who might call me here. If he does, please, please get a telephone number from him where he can be reached."

"Sure, if it's that important to you. What's his name?"

"Eric. Eric Delmont." She was glad she had spoken his name. It made him seem more real to hear his name mentioned in mundane surroundings. Most of the time, he seemed a figment of her imagination.

Monica leaned back into her chair and smirked. "Oh, yes . . . there is one more thing. Lucky, lucky lady . . . you're going on a trip."

"A trip?" Jenny found Monica extremely irritating at times. She couldn't just come out and say anything plainly. Everything had to be developed into a three-act drama.

"Talk to the boss. He's in his office chewing the end off his cigar. The man's in a filthy mood this morning. And he's waiting for you, love," Monica said melodiously.

Hesitantly Jenny left her desk and knocked lightly on Mr. Farrar's office door.

When she emerged fifteen minutes later, her head swam with orders and counterorders. She was leaving that day for Morocco. She had always hoped she'd be able to travel as part of her job at the travel agency, and now, at last, her chance had come. Jenny could feel the excitement welling up inside her.

But what of Eric? He might call while she was away. There was no need to worry, she reassured herself. Monica would take the message and she'd call him later when she returned.

By midafternoon she had packed her suitcase. She left hurried messages for her professors at art school, informing them she'd be away from class and would make up her lessons when she returned.

Mr. Farrar had arranged for her flight, given her explicit instructions on what she was to do for him when in Morocco, and insisted she take down the name and address of a dear friend of his in Marrakesh, Countess Isobel Sevigny. Should Jenny have any problems, she was to call the countess immediately.

THE DC-9 AIRCRAFT LANDED smoothly in Casablanca. It was still early evening and lights from the large, cosmopolitan city flickered against the waning rose-colored sunset.

She had been instructed to spend the night at one of the modern hotels fronting the Atlantic, then leave for Marrakesh the following morning.

Her taxi passed down Avenue Hassan II. Gleaming new buildings lined either side of the street, attesting to the city's modern flavor. Workers had begun to leave their offices and shops for the day, and soon the streets were snarled with stop-and-go traffic.

The cab now crawled slowly among the other vehicles, and from her open window Jenny could hear music from the restaurants and the sidewalk cafés. Every conceivable kind of music assailed her ears—flamenco guitars, gypsy violins, the strains of French and American rock.

International flavor aside, she was soon to find out there was no point in planning an evening on the town. The desk manager at her hotel advised her, somewhat smugly, she thought, that the city's streets became deserted at night. In fact, buses stopped running at nine in the evening. "Tomorrow is a working day," he boasted, as if afraid tourists like Jenny would think his country a nation of nomadic camel drivers.

The hotel was modern and clean. Her room had a private bath and a balcony that opened onto the beach. One of the hotel staff had left a Paris newspaper on her dresser and for want of anything better to do, Jenny lay down on her bed and began to leaf through it.

The headlines were typical—unrest in all parts of the world. She sighed, and was about to put the paper down and have a bath, when a caption caught her eye.

The article was datelined Morocco—Casablanca, to be exact. The thirty-five-year-old daughter of a deposed South American dictator had been found unconscious in her hotel suite earlier that day. Two men—one short and swarthy, the other tall and blond—had broken into her suite while she had been at dinner. She had returned unexpectedly to find them removing her jewelry from the safe that was furnished with her deluxe suite. When she had struggled, one of the men had held her at bay with a gun. By accident it had discharged, wounding her seriously. Several hours later she was discovered by one of the hotel's staff. Although she had lost a lot of blood, her doctors felt she would recover. Her jewels—ill-gotten in the first place, according to some people—were gone.

Jenny put the newspaper down on the dresser.

She eyed the safety lock on her own hotel door. But she didn't have anything to fear; what jewelry did she own?

A thought passed through her mind like a jolt. *The pendant.* Her hand went to her neck and she felt the smooth, cool hardness of the stone. She had no idea how much a necklace like hers was worth, but it would have to be a considerable amount.

Her dreams that night were troubled. Confused images drifted in and out of her consciousness: Eric's handsome face . . . a shadowy image of a dark woman sprawled on the floor, left alone to bleed to death . . . and fleeting impressions of sparkling gems. . . .

Daylight came none too soon.

THE FRAGRANCES OF ORANGE AND thyme, bay leaf and mint, combined in the air to delight the senses.

"*Balek, balek!*" rang masculine voices in the centuries-old *suq*, the Moroccan bazaar, and people scattered to do as they were bid—"make way."

Jenny stepped aside to allow the braying donkeys, and what seemed to be a never ending stream of rickety horse-drawn caleches, to pass.

Earlier Thursday afternoon she had checked into the Dar Saada in Marrakesh. It was located just outside the wall in the medina, the oldest part of the city.

Her purpose for coming to Marrakesh was to approve the hotel for accommodating future charter groups. Mr. Farrar had received heated complaints from some of his best clients regarding conditions at the current hotel they used for tours.

After checking in she had decided to see some of the city while it was still daylight.

Her journey by foot took her through a labyrinth of

winding, snaking streets. Shops, nestled in ancient walls, sold everything from *babouches*—hand-embroidered slippers of leather—to ribbons and birdcages. A street hawker persuaded her to buy almonds, while another merchant pleaded persuasively with her to enter his stall selling spices of ground red and black pepper, cumin, paprika, ginger and mustard seed.

Like a huge, swirling circus, the Marrakesh marketplace dazzled the senses, and Jenny found herself lured deeper and deeper into its fabled square of intrigue.

"Come . . . come . . ." hissed a fortune-teller, a man sitting cross-legged on a reed mat. His hand held an ornate tarot card with a picture of death. The grotesque face on the card seemed to wink lasciviously at her from the shadows that were quickly falling as evening neared.

Jenny recalled from her travel brochures that long ago the square had indeed been a place where death had resided. The heads of rebels and bandits had once been impaled on pointed sticks as a warning to onlookers to conduct themselves with honor and discretion. The "Assembly of the Dead," as it had become known, was still a fearsome place—especially after dark.

She turned down one of the narrow passageways, confident that if she continued in that direction she would find her way back to the main thoroughfare leading to the Dar Saada.

Behind her beat the rhythmic *tam-tams*, signaling the crowds to gather for the afternoon circus held in Djema-El Fna. Women in burnooses passed her by, their heads down, faces unseen, as they hurried with armloads of dough to bake their bread for the evening meal in the public ovens. Dark-eyed men, tanned from the fierce North African sun, passed in groups wearing robes of white or blue or red cotton that swirled gracefully about them. Everywhere there was color and movement.

Jenny's head had begun to ache. The alleyways were narrower now. She should have taken another route, that much was clear, but always it seemed that the next corner would be the one to lead her out of the now terrifying maze and into a recognizable street.

Exhausted, she stopped for a moment, leaning against a crumbling white wall. The street she had turned onto was quiet; few people walked its narrow confines. Compared with the boisterous gaiety near the market, the silence was ominous.

Tomorrow, she decided, she would take a tour of the rest of the city with other visitors. She would not risk becoming lost a second time.

Again she began to walk. Behind her, she heard a scraping sound and turned to look. No one was there.

Holding her purse clutched tightly against her chest, she continued on her way, her heart beating a little faster. Another sound—rushing and furtive. She turned quickly as a tall figure emerged from out of the shadows, looming before her, a white-robed specter with black eyes gleaming in the dim light.

With a sweep of his arm, he pushed her against the wall, her back scraping against the rough plaster. Silently he gestured with his head for her to move toward a narrow, arched gate in the wall. It was several feet away and she stumbled on the uneven cobbles as she was shoved roughly in the directon of the arch. She looked feverishly up and down the alleyway for help. There was no one in sight.

The figure in white backed her into the gate, which opened soundlessly.

She found herself in a small garden—or what had been a

garden at some other time. But she had no time to absorb her surroundings. Without being asked, Jenny presented the figure her purse, holding it out to him with both hands. The man took it, dipping his hand inside to pull out her wallet.

Briefly he glanced at her identification—looking up at her for a moment, as if an idea had crossed his mind—then searched for money, taking the small amount she carried with her.

Her heart pounding with fear, Jenny remained quiet, not daring to speak or make a movement, lest she inadvertently anger him. Slowly he approached her, his nose and mouth covered, displaying only the bright dark eyes that peered malevolently at her in the dusk.

Suddenly his arm shot out and he caught her by one shoulder, forcing her toward him. His hand moved to her throat, and with a gasp of horror Jenny tried to jerk away. In vain.

He's going to kill me, Jenny thought, frozen with terror.

He'd strangle her and leave her forgotten and alone, just as the dictator's daughter had been left alone to die in a hotel room. Only this time there would be no one to rescue the unfortunate victim.

But instead of feeling a pressure against her throat as the man leaned forward, she felt the roughness of calloused fingers moving against her skin. Jenny suddenly realized what it was he wanted. He was attempting to undo the necklace—the beautiful emerald pendant that Eric had given her so lovingly only a few days before. But she didn't dare try to stop him. Instead, she gave a shudder and closed her eyes as the thief completed his task.

Within a minute he had managed to unlatch the delicate

clasp. Acting quickly, no movement wasted, he dropped the necklace into a small leather pouch he wore looped around his belt with a drawstring, and as suddenly as he had appeared he left.

For long, tension-filled minutes, Jenny waited alone in the courtyard garden overgrown with vegetation. She was still alive; she hadn't been hurt. But she had been numb with fear, and her heart still pounded with a desperate momentum.

She would have to leave. But the man could be waiting for her somewhere in the shadows beyond the wall. No, that was unlikely, she reasoned. Had he wanted to harm her, he'd already had the opportunity. She was safe—at least from him.

But there could be others like him, or worse, posted along the treacherous corridors of Marrakesh waiting to take their unsuspecting prey. Ultimately, of course, she had no choice. No matter how dangerous, there was only one way she'd be able to get back to the Dar Saada, and that was by opening the gate and once again entering the street outside.

Two hours later, both mentally and physically exhausted, she arrived back at the hotel. The heel on one of her shoes had broken on the cobbles; she had entered the hotel lobby with shoe in hand. No doubt to the staff and other guests of the hotel, she presented a curious sight as she limped through the foyer. But she was oblivious to their stares and whispers. All she wanted was to get back to her room. Only there, behind a locked door, would she feel safe.

Her room was in darkness when she opened the door. Quickly she turned on the wall switch. A bright globe instantly cast light from the ceiling to every corner of the room. She fastened both locks on her door and checked to make certain the sliding window leading to the balcony was secure.

Satisfied at last, she flung herself onto the bed and gave way to uncontrollable sobbing. The necklace—Eric's beautiful necklace—was gone. It had been in his family for generations and now, after only a few days, she'd managed to lose it. And she had only herself to blame. It wasn't as if she hadn't known that a young woman alone was an easy target for the unscrupulous; not just in Marrakesh, but in any major metropolis. What a fool she'd been to wear it—an open invitation even to the most petty of crooks. Why, oh, why, hadn't she simply put it in the hotel safe or, better still, left it in Paris? But she knew only too well why she hadn't; Eric had told her never to take it off, until . . . .

Bit by bit her flood of tears slowed; then they finally stopped, and she began to think more coherently. She knew it would be futile to contact the police; there were thousands of petty thieves in a city the size of Marrakesh. But she'd have to make some attempt to retrieve the necklace, or she'd never be able to face Eric again.

Suddenly, she sat up in bed, remembering.

Mr. Farrar had given her the address of his friend, the Countess Isobel Sevigny, to call should she have any problem. And if this didn't constitute a problem, she didn't know what did.

Fired up by the thought of positive action, she grabbed the receiver from the telephone in the room and urged the hotel operator to find the countess's telephone number. To no avail. The countess had an unlisted number. *I'll visit her tomorrow*, Jenny thought. *I'm sure she'll be able to advise me.*

THE CAB DRIVER KNEW immediately where she wanted to go. He sped through the streets at breakneck pace, miraculously managing to avoid pedestrians and other vehicles as he careened around corners.

At the ride's end Jenny found herself deposited in front of the fortresslike walls of a castle she learned later was four hundred years old—the residence of the countess. Jenny only hoped that Mr. Farrar's friend would be home.

A manservant answered the steady ring of large bells tied to the end of a rope. He spoke French less than fluently but seemed to have little trouble understanding Jenny, and when she'd finished explaining who she was he bid her enter.

She followed him past a long rectangular reflecting pool containing a small fountain in its center. White arched doors surrounded the pool in the central courtyard and potted plants lodged beneath the tile roof's overhang.

Her guide left her in a large room with white walls and electric ceiling fans. They rotated noiselessly, the breeze created by their wooden blades causing the fronds of the potted palms to sway and shiver. It was a cool room, protected from the heat outside by its thick walls.

Colorful upholstery made of Indian, Persian and Moroccan textiles covered fashionable overstuffed chairs and sofas. Brass objects gleamed on low tables and antique chests were partially open, exhibiting museum quality artifacts. Jenny looked around her in awe, feeling suddenly nervous as she realized how vastly wealthy must be the woman she'd come to see. Uninvited guests would not be expected, or appreciated, in a place like this.

A white louvered door swung open at the far end of the room and a woman appeared wearing a long, flowing caftan of striped, raw silk. Her hair was rich black and was pulled back severely into a knot at the nape of her neck. Her skin, tanned a deep brown, gave her light brown eyes the appearance of amber.

"I am the Countess Isobel Sevigny," she announced proudly. "Why have you come?"

Neither her haughty demeanor nor her cold tone did anything to alleviate Jenny's nervousness. "I—I'm Jennifer Gordon," she stammered. "I was . . . given your name by my employer, Mr. Yves Farrar."

"Yves?" To Jenny's great relief, the countess's face changed immediately. She was no longer aloof; in fact, her face shone with the warmth of a pleasant memory.

"Mr. Farrar told me to contact you if I found myself in any difficulty," explained Jenny, feeling a great deal more at ease.

The older woman's face clouded. "You're in trouble?" she inquired, turning her head away, as if listening for an eavesdropper. "What kind of trouble?"

"I've been robbed."

"Of your money? Your passport? What has been taken?"

"A necklace."

"I see." The countess seemed to consider the answer. Lowering herself to one of the cushioned seats, she patted an adjacent chair for Jenny to do likewise.

"Tell me about it," the countess said gently, and Jenny recounted the incident, shivering at the memory. When she had finished the countess waited a moment before she spoke, then said, "This is a very large city; there are many people here—some not so nice. Dangerous, you might have to say." Her tongue tripped slowly over the word dangerous.

Jenny was beginning to realize how foolish she had been

to think that the countess, or anyone, could possibly help her retrieve the necklace.

"Please," she said, beginning to rise. "I'm terribly sorry to have bothered you with this, countess. Of course it's absolutely apparent now that it would be impossible to find my necklace."

"Impossible?" echoed the countess in obvious astonishment. "What is this word, impossible?"

"There's no hope—"

"Impossible is a word that I have long since removed from my vocabulary," interrupted the countess firmly. "It does not exist. Difficult—yes; that word may exist. And in this case it may be difficult to obtain the return of your necklace."

"You mean that you think you can actually find some way to get my necklace back?" Jenny asked, incredulous that she had heard correctly.

The countess appeared thoughtful. She moved her eyes over objects in her room, as if weighing information from the past.

"This is something that I would not like to become involved in. I tell you this, only because I want you to inform Yves what I have done for you. I do it not for you, but for him. We go back many years together, and if a friend cannot be counted upon—then what use is friendship?"

Jenny remained silent. It was apparent that the countess spoke only to herself as she relived moments of a bygone relationship.

The countess rose and walked to the wall, where she took hold of a long, flat woven cord and pulled three times. Within seconds a muscular young man appeared inside the doorway of the room.

In a dialect Jenny could not understand, the countess spoke to him, and his eyes darted from the older woman to Jenny, seeing everything in one glance. He spoke back to the countess quickly and seriously, then backed from the room, pausing to dip his head slightly as a parting gesture of respect to the older woman.

"Stay in your hotel this afternoon. Today my friend will come to your room with the necklace."

"How is that possible?" Jenny whispered.

"It is possible, because it is not impossible," the woman instructed, again more to herself than to Jenny. Then she raised her head and spoke more directly. "This is a city of secrets. I have lived here many years and have learned a great many of its secrets. Look around you. When I came here I had nothing but the clothes on my back and a husband who had disgraced himself in France . . . and who was soon to die with a saber in his back from committing another impropriety in a city whose inhabitants are not as lenient as those of Paris. Since that time, I have done well, no?"

Jenny followed the countess's gaze, touching upon the magnificent antiques and ending at her wrist, from which dangled a bracelet encrusted with jewels.

"You have a most beautiful home, countess, and some very beautiful objects around. They must give you great pleasure."

The countess didn't answer. Rather, she just looked weary, and slowly walked back to Jenny. "When you get your necklace, it would be wise to leave the city as soon as possible. Just a precaution, you understand. Tell your employer, Mr. Farrar, that he is always welcome in Marrakesh, especially here at the home of his old friend."

The countess walked from the room, leaving Jenny

alone. Almost immediately, the servant who had opened the door for her reappeared. She followed him to the street entrance.

Outside once again, she heard the final sound of the iron doors being locked in place. The countess took precautions to protect herself. And perhaps, thought Jenny, there was ample cause for her to do so.

At HALF-PAST THREE, a light knock sounded against Jenny's door. Cautiously she opened it, keeping the chain lock in place while peering through the narrow crack.

The young man she had seen earlier, when he had been called into the room by the countess, stood in the hall. His white *djellabas* bore dirt stains, testimony of some recent scuffle. On the side of his face there was a nasty-looking scratch, from which some blood still trickled.

Quickly Jenny opened the door wide, but the man remained standing in the hall. His hand disappeared into the folds of his garment and Jenny gasped in delighted disbelief as it reappeared holding Eric's necklace.

Slowly she took it from him, staring at it with amazement. And with equal amazement she looked up, searching his face. His dark eyes were without expression. She knew enough to be sure he didn't speak French or English, so there was no way of thanking him properly, or of asking him how the necklace had been retrieved, although by his appearance she knew it hadn't been easy.

"Wait," she said in French and walked to her dresser, opening her purse and removing a handful of money from her wallet, earlier converted from traveler's checks after the robbery. When she turned back, the man had gone.

Three hours later she dressed for dinner. Although she would have preferred to eat a quiet meal in her room, part of her job required her to investigate as much of the hotel's operation as possible.

However, the necklace posed a problem. After her terrifying experience of the previous day, she knew it was foolhardy even to consider wearing it. Without question it served as a lure to unscrupulous people, but Eric's memory *"Put it on. And don't ever take it off. Not until I replace it with something else."*

It was tempting fate, but she needed to feel the pendant about her neck. It had become a part of her now, perhaps because it made her feel a part of Eric's life. Besides, surely she would be safe in the hotel dining room.

The dress she selected to wear to dinner was a plain, light yellow jersey. The combination of the dress and her fair hair made her look soft and vulnerable, and as she entered the lavish Moroccan restaurant, heads turned to follow her progress to the table.

The room was filled to capacity with diners talking and laughing over cocktails and low tables piled high with sumptuous displays of the native cuisine.

She picked up the dinner menu and pored over it for some minutes, finding it impossible to choose among the many exotic dishes. The waiter thoughtfully suggested some typical Moroccan dishes for her to try, and he described each as he brought them. First she was presented with a pot of thick and aromatic soup, called *harira*. That was followed by *poulet au citron*, chicken with olives and pickled lemons. She tasted the *bastilla*, a poultry pie seasoned with cinnamon and lemon, and was told no meal in Morocco was complete without the national dish, *couscous*, steamed grains surrounded by vegetables, raisins and chunks of lamb.

Jenny had barely finished dining when the lights of the restaurant dimmed and she could hear music, softly at first, then more loudly as four male musicians assembled at the edge of a small cleared space in the center of the room. Spectators stared in fascination at the shapely young woman who then entered the room and began to undulate in time to the *oud*, an Arab flute.

The woman's hair beneath her swirling veils appeared to be as coal-black and shiny as the eyes that flashed provocatively above the edge of the gauze that covered the lower portion of her face. Mesmerized, everyone in the room followed the dancer's sensual, swaying movements.

At a table across the room, a match flared as someone lighted a cigarette. Momentarily distracted from the dance by the sudden flash of light, Jenny glanced in its direction.

What she saw across the room made her gasp in astonishment. Barely distinguishable in the subdued lighting, sat a man who looked identical to Eric Delmont.

She strained to see better, certain she had to be mistaken. The coincidence of Eric's being in the same restaurant in the same country was too improbable to be possible—yet, as the countess had so forcefully pointed out, nothing was impossible.

Much to her annoyance, her view was obscured somewhat by a heavy-set man and his equally plump female companion, both moving constantly as they positioned themselves for a more advantageous view of the entertainment.

The belly dancer moved through the room, stopping at tables, swaying in time to the *oud* and the steady beat of the percussion instruments, as she allowed customers to reward her artful performance by placing money into the

top of her bodice and into the spangled band at the top of
her skirt. She moved again; this time toward the man who
looked like Eric.

Jenny waited, barely daring to breathe, as the woman
hovered by his table. At last she moved away, leaving him
in clear view.

He was with an older woman, not unattractive from
what Jenny could see, but not a young beauty like Candy
McManus, either. Eric—if indeed it was Eric—seemed absorbed in something she was saying. A moment later, they
both stood. The woman smiled, and the man who looked
like Eric leaned over and kissed her hand before leading her
from the table.

Without moving, Jenny followed them with her eyes,
watching as they crossed to the door that led from the
restaurant into the hotel lobby.

She couldn't be absolutely certain—not without a closer
look—but from where she was sitting everything about
him told her he was Eric. The cut of his clothes was expensive and continental, his walk was smooth and athletic,
his every movement was spare and assured. If it wasn't
Eric, then Eric had a double—a brother who was a twin.

But, no; that *was* impossible. Eric had told her that he
was an only child. There would be no reason for him to lie
to her.

Something—she wasn't sure what—had made her hang
back rather than rush to his table and declare her presence.
Now that he had left the room, she realized she had been
foolish not to approach him.

She motioned to her waiter to bring the check. Quickly
she signed her name, billing the meal to her room number.
In a minute she had left the restaurant and entered the
lobby.

The woman was at the cashier's desk, talking to the manager of the hotel. Her companion was nowhere in sight.

Pretending to look through a rack of airline schedules in a stand against the wall, Jenny kept her eyes on the other woman. Eric would undoubtedly be back. It would be less awkward if he approached her, rather than she him. She waited.

The manager and the woman finished their conversation, and he turned and disappeared into a room behind the counter. A moment later he reappeared, carrying a small gray sack, which seemed to be made out of velvet, and a flat case in a shiny, silklike material.

The woman slipped the box and the bag into her purse and walked to the hotel's front door. Jenny started after her.

Passing through the double glass doors leading to the street, the woman walked ahead to a red sports car idling in front of the hotel. She opened the passenger's door and got inside.

This time Jenny was certain; as she looked through the glass doors, she could clearly see the man in the driver's seat. It was Eric Delmont.

Jenny's first reaction to her extraordinary discovery was one of puzzlement. What was Eric doing in Marrakesh? And why hadn't he told her he was coming?

Puzzlement quickly gave way to anger. During dinner at Chez Cary, she had been lured into believing she meant something to him. And now, just a few days later, here he was wining and dining another woman! After all she'd gone through for his wretched necklace, too!

Here Jenny checked her thoughts, realizing she probably wasn't being very fair. After all, she still didn't know what, if anything, Eric did for a living, and it was entirely possible the woman she'd just seen him with was no more than a business associate.

Nevertheless, she was jealous, and there was still a dull ache in her heart when she went to bed that night.

SATURDAY MORNING DAWNED blue and gold and brilliant. Strands of white clouds moved overhead in slow, steady streams of trailing white lace. The air was fresh and clean, free of the dust that would soon rise as the city's activities progressed to the frenetic pace of daily living.

Jenny gazed out the window of the tour bus. It was crowded, its passengers preoccupied with loading and unloading expensive German and Japanese cameras as they prepared to capture the next landmark for posterity.

Her plane left at two o'clock that afternoon. She'd barely have time to return to the hotel after the tour to get her suitcases. But she was glad of the rush; that way she didn't have time to think about Eric. Anyway, it was foolish to dwell upon the mysteries that surrounded him. Tomorrow she would be back at work and Monica would hand her a number where she could reach him. She'd simply ask him point-blank why he had disappeared the night at the restaurant and what he was doing in Morocco. . . .

The woman sitting beside her let out a long sigh. Jenny smiled, but the woman shook her head and shook the newspaper in her hands.

"Look," she said, pointing to the picture of a woman. "You can't be too careful."

The picture the woman pointed to was an old one, not particularly clear, but Jenny could still recognize the face of the lady she had seen with Eric in the restaurant the previous evening.

"She was robbed last night," the woman beside her said, and chucked indignantly. "Right in the Dar Saada Hotel. I'm staying there myself," she added, as if proud to be connected with the headlines.

"What happened?" Jenny asked, not really wanting to know, but compelled to ask nevertheless. The thought that Eric might be connected with yet another robbery filled her with dread; she turned her head to look out the window, afraid to face her companion.

"The newspaper says the woman took her jewelry out of the hotel's safe to wear to a party last night. She returned late, and was too tired to bother putting it away, so she kept it right there with her in her suite. Locked her door, too," the woman related. "When she awoke this morning, it was gone. All of it."

Jenny tried to relax. There was no reason to suspect Eric. The robbery had happened after the woman had returned to the hotel. What did it matter if she had been with him earlier? Anyone could have broken into her room while she slept.

Anyone . . . including Eric.

Jenny pushed the unwelcome thought from her mind and forced herself to concentrate on the twelfth-century Koutoubya Mosque.

Chapter 4

As she entered the office on Tuesday morning, having had Monday off for New Year's, Marrakesh seemed no more than a distant dream.

Monica was already hard at work; Mr. Farrar was busy opening boxes of brochures that just arrived by delivery truck.

"Jennifer!" he cried when he saw her, dropping what he was doing. "How was the trip?"

"Fine," she answered. "I'll type up a full report on the Dar Saada. And—tell you about my other adventure."

"Good . . . good," he said, and dove back into the boxes of brochures.

The telephone rang and Monica answered.

"Yes, she's here."

Jenny's heart stood still. *Eric*, she thought. *Please, please let it be Eric.*

Monica put the telephone on hold. "It's for you," she said.

Jenny rushed to her desk and picked up the receiver. "Hello, this is Jenny."

"Hi! It's me, Anne. How about lunch today?"

"Oh . . . Anne." She tried to disguise her disappointment. "Yes, that would be nice. Lunch at twelve?"

"The usual place."

"See you there," she said, and hung up.

Mr. Farrar had left the room, happily transferring two boxes of advertising material to his private office.

"By the way, did I have any calls while I was gone, Monica?" asked Jenny.

"Calls?" Monica looked up from her work, an expression of surprise on her face. "Yes, of course. I put all your messages right there on your desk."

"Yes, I saw those," Jenny replied. "But . . . well I was just wondering if I had any other calls. Maybe a personal one?"

Monica shook her head. "All your calls are right there on your desk," she repeated, a trace of reproach in her voice, for her efficiency being challenged.

So Eric hadn't called. Dejected, Jenny slumped into her chair. There was no way that she would be able to reach him. All she could do was wait. And hope.

Anne met her at the café where they usually met for lunch. In the warmer months, they would sit on the terrace outside. During the winter they dined indoors, preferring a small table located near the fireplace.

Jenny felt a small stab of jealousy as she entered the restaurant and saw Anne, already seated, looking positively radiant with happiness. Over lunch, she bubbled with enthusiasm, insisting she was in love. The boring viscount, she explained had called her and invited her on a hike in the country over the weekend.

"But I thought you hated hiking," objected Jenny, breaking up a piece of French bread.

"I do," admitted her friend cheerily. "But I adore money

and the viscount is very, very rich," she elaborated, waving a bread stick in the air to punctuate her statement.

Ordinarily Jenny would have laughed, but now she was too busy thinking. "Anne," she said, looking pensive, "I've got to find Eric Delmont—the man I met at the Christmas Eve party."

"So? What's the big deal? Look him up in the telephone directory."

"I already tried that. He's not listed."

Anne was quiet for a moment, then said, "I get it. If he was invited to that party then he'd have to be pretty important, and pretty important people don't exactly advertise their telephone numbers or addresses."

"I've really got to get in touch with him."

"Hasn't he called you?"

"No. We had dinner last Tuesday night and he gave me this." Jenny exposed the pendant, which she had tucked inside the neckline of her dress.

"Oh . . . it's beautiful," Anne breathed reverently, her dark eyes dancing with unsuppressed admiration.

"I know. But I want to give it back."

"You want to . . . ? Why? You're mad! Or did that hot sun in Morocco affect your mind?"

"Let's just say I don't feel comfortable keeping it. It's too valuable a gift to accept. If I lost it—and I almost did once—I'd never be able to forgive myself."

And besides, she thought miserably, *there's no way to know if Eric was telling the truth about the necklace being in his family.* There was another way it could have come into his possession. . . .

Anne drummed her fingers against the tabletop. "Hmm," she said, "I suppose there's one way we could find out how to reach him."

"How?"

"Go back to Château des Fleurs; ask the marquis. It was his party."

"Of course! It's a marvelous idea!" exclaimed Jenny delightedly, feeling as if a weight had suddenly been lifted from her.

As soon as she got Eric's telephone number she'd call him, arrange a meeting and confront him with all the mysteries that plagued her. He'd explain everything to her satisfaction and her worries would no doubt appear ridiculous in the light of truth. In fact, she'd probably laugh about it afterward.

"We can go on Saturday," Anne said. "I'll pick you up at ten. That way we'll arrive at the château just in time to be invited to lunch." She giggled and winked mischievously.

THE MARQUIS WAS SHORT and balding. Jenny guessed him to be about forty. He dressed impeccably, but his clothes were meant for someone of Eric's height and athletic build.

He was at once cordial and reserved when they appeared unannounced on his doorstep. Jenny supposed it was more the novelty of having anyone be so guileless, rather than the desire to be of assistance to them, that prompted him to invite them in for a light lunch.

Anne, on the other hand, was under the impression that she had maneuvered the invitation herself, and whispered superlatives about her cunning whenever the marquis was preoccupied with a household matter.

Light finger sandwiches were served, along with tea and biscuits. Anne munched happily, looking over the room's decor, but Jenny was uncomfortable, finding it difficult to keep up the stilted conversation.

"You say you're a friend of Rita Baldridge?" the marquis asked Anne.

"Yes, Rita and I have known each other for several

years," she answered truthfully, for in fact she had done the woman's hair once a week for two years.

It was obvious that Anne was fooling no one with her airs. The marquis looked mildly amused at the pretense, but only mildly, Jenny judged. She decided to put an end to the charade.

"Marquis, I've been trying to get in touch with a gentleman I met at your party."

The marquis raised an eyebrow and gave the slightest of shrugs, not unnoticed by his guest.

She knew what he was thinking; that she was probably a lovesick schoolgirl, trying to chase down a man who had no interest in her. Embarrassed, she gestured to the pendant around her neck to lend herself credibility.

"The person I need to contact gave me this."

"It's very lovely," commented the marquis, suddenly looking at her with more interest.

"Yes. And valuable, I'm sure. That's why I want to return it."

"Really? How unusual," he said, an ironic smile playing on the corners of his mouth. "And what might be your generous friend's name?"

"Eric Delmont."

Jenny could have sworn there was a slight flicker of recognition in his eyes as she spoke the name. But perhaps she'd been mistaken, for an instant later his face was devoid of all expression.

"What a pity," he said, with a languid wave of his hand. "You've wasted your time, I'm afraid. I don't believe that I know any Eric Delmont."

Anne looked quickly at Jenny.

"But you must," Anne insisted. "He was at your party."

The marquis returned her challenge with a prolonged

stare. "Perhaps he was. But surely you can understand that anyone in my position who gives a party as large as the one held Christmas Eve is fair game for celebrity hounds—and others," he added pointedly.

"But this is different," Jenny said emphatically, choosing to ignore the implication of the last remark. "I'm sure that this man is not the type of person to crash a party like yours. He's refined and elegant, and I'm certain he has money of his own. There'd be no need."

The marquis folded his arms across his chest and threw back his head as he gave a light laugh. "My dear girl," he said, not unkindly, but making his point nevertheless, "in my circle, there are many men and women who are extremely accomplished at passing themselves off for something that they're not. Perhaps you should take heed."

Jenny felt physically ill. It was the one thing she had not wanted to hear. "I'm sorry, but I just don't believe that Eric Delmont is that sort of a person," she said softly.

The marquis looked thoughtful. He stared at her intently, as if on the verge of making a decision, then turned his attention to a misplaced thread on his tweed jacket. He picked it off and said, "I suggest that you wait for the gentleman to call you."

Anne pursed her lips, obviously finding it difficult to allow such a patronizing remark to pass without her comment.

Jenny rose from her seat; the marquis followed her lead.

"If you remember Mr. Delmont at some later date, marquis, perhaps you'd be so good as to mention my visit."

"Certainly."

"Your help would be very much appreciated."

The marquis saw them to the front door. Anne looked at him with daggers in her eyes. Jenny merely looked sad.

"Miss Gordon?" the marquis called, just as she stepped across the threshold.

"Yes?"

"I'm sorry I can't help you."

Did she imagine it, or did the marquis place added emphasis on the word "can't"?

Anne was spitting mad on the way home. "I could have scratched his eyes out," she seethed. "You know what he thought, don't you?"

"He thought I had a lot of nerve coming to him, and he thought I had a lot of nerve chasing a man down, and he thought I was stupid to have believed a romantic line I heard at a party," replied Jenny matter-of-factly.

"He's the one with a lot of nerve," returned her friend angrily. "How dare he talk to us like that. . . ."

"He could be right, you know," Jenny pointed out with a sigh.

"How can you say that? You're supposed to be in love." Anne looked aghast. Her foot trounced down harder on the gas pedal.

"Oh, Annie, don't you see? The marquis has seen things like this happen a hundred times. Eric could have been anyone at all. He could have been a fortune hunter looking for a rich woman. He might have been there to make some sort of business connection with a rich industrialist. He could have been any kind of an opportunist." She stopped short of pointing out the most obvious conclusion: *Eric might have been there to steal jewelry.*

"All right, I'll admit you've got a point here and there," said Anne grudgingly.

"Except . . ." Jenny said slowly, suddenly remembering the expression on the marquis's face when she first mentioned Eric's name, "I think the marquis was lying. I think he does know Eric."

"Then why wouldn't he tell you how to get in touch with him?"

"I don't know. Maybe it was because he really believed I was a golddigger."

Anne snorted. "Ha! You a golddigger? That's a laugh."

"Wait a minute!" Jenny's voice was sharp as she sat up straighter in her seat. "The marquis *was* lying to us. He *does* know Eric." She turned excitedly toward her friend. "I'm certain of it, Anne."

Anne looked puzzled. "What do you mean?" she queried. "I don't get it."

"Don't you remember? The night of the party we walked past the marquis and Eric. They were standing by the door to the drawing room."

Anne's face lighted up in sudden understanding. "Oh, yes . . . now I remember."

"And they weren't just standing side by side. They were talking to each other."

Anne furrowed her brow, thinking back to the night of the party. "The marquis said something about having to be careful. He said something else, too. What was it?"

"Danger," Jenny replied slowly. "It was something about being careful . . . because there was . . . danger."

"You're right," Anne said thoughtfully, turning to her friend. "Do you think Eric's involved with something really serious?"

Jenny sighed and leaned her head back into the headrest. "Oh, Anne, I don't know what to think anymore. There are so many questions, and no answers for them."

Anne slowed the car. A few yards farther on, she pulled

it off to the side of the road, braked to a halt and turned off the engine.

"Okay, Jenny," she said, turning to face her friend squarely, "I know you're interested in this man Eric Delmont. I know he's attractive and romantic and all that. That's super. But, listen, friend . . . there's something going on here that's a little bit unsettling. Jen, you could be in real danger yourself if you get involved with this man any more than you already are."

Jenny turned her face away and looked out the window. The meadow beyond was dotted with fruit trees, their branches barren of leaves, their gnarled trunks contorted from years of withstanding the elements.

Without Eric in her life, she suddenly felt desolate. But at the same time she knew Anne was right. Eric could be involved in something dangerous, and her own life might be drawn into the unsavory intrigue if she continued to see him. But without Eric . . . .

She knew it wasn't possible to make Anne understand the intensity of the emotions that had passed between them the two nights they had been together, just as she knew that no matter what Eric Delmont was involved in, no matter if he were thief—or worse—he did care for her.

"Jenny? Are you listening to me?"

"What?"

"I've been talking to you for the last five minutes, giving you my valuable advice, I might add, and I don't believe you've heard a word I've said."

"I know what you said, and you're right," admitted Jenny.

"You really think so?"

"Absolutely. Only, it doesn't make any difference."

Anne shook her head. "That's what I was afraid of," she sighed.

"I've got to find Eric," Jenny insisted. "I want to give him back the necklace."

"Well, while you're at it, why don't you ask him why he left you those two times, and why each time there had been a jewel heist?"

"I promise. The moment I see Eric, I'll ask him."

Anne restarted the car. Before pulling onto the road, she looked over at Jenny and said, "I just hope that by the time you do, it won't be too late."

Chapter 5

The alarm sounded, but it was unnecessary. Jenny was already wide awake, thinking. She reached across the bed to the clock radio on her night stand, stilled its shrill buzzer, and sat up.

Monday. Again.

She hadn't spoken to Eric for nearly two weeks. Already it seemed as if months had passed since she had been with him at the restaurant.

She dragged herself out of the warm bed and walked across the hardwood floor to her closet in search of something to wear to work. The wood felt icy under her feet, but her thoughts occupied her mind and the slight discomfort went almost unnoticed.

So much had happened, and yet nothing had happened. In nearly two weeks Eric hadn't had the time—or desire, it seemed—to call.

Jenny rifled through her closet and selected a navy blue skirt. She matched it with a red and white blouse, then decided she wasn't in the mood for a skirt, after all. In fact, she wasn't in the mood for anything. The skirt and blouse were returned to the closet.

Was she such a fool that she couldn't tell the difference between a man who wanted her because it boosted his ego to be with a pretty woman at dinner, a woman who was suitable for brief public appearances, but not to be taken seriously—and a man who wanted her as a whole person, to be loved and treated with consideration?

Had she no better judgment than to believe lies from a pair of deep blue eyes across a candlelit table? Apparently not.

Her eyes rested on the white dress she had worn the night at the Chez Cary when she had dined with Eric. Remembering, she took it from the rack and held it against her, as if trying to recapture the evening through the feel of the fabric.

At least she still had the pendant to prove Eric had meant what he'd said that night. Surely he would never have parted with the necklace unless he truly cared for her. Or hadn't it meant anything to him? Had it perhaps come from a dark hotel room, the property of some wealthy unsuspecting stranger?

Jenny hated herself for the ugly thought, but she had to be realistic. She had to stop playing the innocent, wined and dined and romanced into believing she had met the great love of her life.

Only . . . she did believe it. She did love Eric. Of that, at least, she was certain. And the rest? That she would just have to discover.

She'd wear the white dress again—if for no other reason than sheer obstinacy.

The irony of how quickly emotions can change and alter one's entire perspective on life was not lost on her. When she had worn the dress to have dinner with Eric she had been on cloud nine; this week she had plummeted rudely back to earth.

Wearing the white dress, she'd need to change purses. She reached up to the shelf in her closet and removed the small clutch bag she had carried the night of her dinner at Chez Cary.

Forgotten for two weeks, a small flat object lay undisturbed at the bottom of the purse. The matchbook that Eric had given her when it had fallen from his jacket pocket had completely slipped her mind. At the time, she had admired only briefly the intricate design on its cover, meaning to look at it more closely when she returned home.

Now, holding it up to the light from her window, she examined the gold engraving on the felt. The matches came from the Pierre Hotel in Paris.

Her hand closed over the matches. She knew the place—the Pierre was an older, established hotel, well-known for catering to foreign movie stars, international diplomats and old-guard wealth.

The name of the hotel was synonymous with discretion. Reputedly two of its floors contained private apartments, maintained as permanent residences by undisclosed dignitaries who didn't mind paying exorbitant fees for the tight-lipped service the hotel afforded.

Either Eric had been at the Pierre, or he had been around someone who had stayed there. Perhaps he actually resided there himself. It was a slim chance, maybe only a wild hope, but it was a possibility she was not prepared to overlook.

THE WALL CLOCK in the office struck nine as Jenny opened the door to the travel agency.

"Congratulations," remarked Monica casually. "You made it."

Jenny ignored the somewhat sarcastic greeting, hung up her coat and headed for her desk.

"Did you have a nice weekend?" Monica asked suddenly.

Jenny turned, surprised by the question. Her co-worker wasn't in the habit of making pleasant small talk. But, of course, it was probably obvious to her that there was something wrong. And Jenny knew from previous experience that Monica was always interested in other people's troubles. Perhaps they helped her forget her own occasionally.

Jenny sat down and looked squarely at her co-worker, who waited with an air of undisguised expectancy. "It was . . . interesting," she said, thinking of her visit to the marquis on Saturday.

Monica was obviously disappointed by the response. "Not . . . romantic?" she queried.

"Is there something specific you want to know about my weekend?" Jenny asked, coldly. After all, it was really none of Monica's business.

"Just trying to be friendly, that's all," Monica replied, affecting a tone of injured innocence. "You seemed to be so upset last week, I thought things might have improved over the weekend."

"Why would they have improved? You know very well why I've been upset."

"Presumably you haven't received your call?" inquired Monica airily.

"No, I haven't received it," Jenny replied crossly.

"Or—have I? She searched her co-worker's face carefully for the answer to her question.

"You've got lots of calls; they're all on your desk. Don't be so greedy."

Jenny went through the stack of pink messages on her spindle. There was nothing from Eric, but then she hadn't really expected there to be.

"Maybe he isn't going to call you. Did you ever think of that?" Monica leaned back in her chair, a trace of amusement on her face.

Ignoring the bait, Jenny took an invoice from her desk tray and began to review the charges.

"Could it be that you aren't that attractive to him?"

Smiling sweetly in response, Jenny looked up for a moment, then returned to her work. The calculator buzzed as she entered the various amounts into its memory bank.

Monica raised her voice to compensate for the noise. "Anyway, it's comforting to know I'm not the only one who spends her weekends alone, waiting for the phone to ring."

"Well, at least you're fortunate enough to have a phone at home," retorted Jenny. "I don't, so I have to find other things to occupy my time."

"True," admitted Monica, rather reluctantly Jenny though. "So, if Eric Delmont calls, he'll have to reach you here. And I answer the phone. That's one call I'll be looking forward to."

Jenny's only response was to hit the total button on her calculator.

MR. FARRAR HÀD ALLOWED HER to leave early. At three o'clock, Jenny hailed a cab outside the travel agency and gave the driver the Pierre's address.

Twenty minutes later she walked into the hotel lobby and approached the polished mahogany counter that had registered such notables as Winston Churchill and Princess Grace of Monaco.

Thick carpet covered the floor, muffling the footsteps of patrons who crossed the wide octagonal room, their voices low and muted as they spoke of deals—both business and personal—yet to be consummated.

Jenny thought she recognized a blond American actress, noted not only for the roles she played, but for her amorous adventures offscreen, as well. Anne had said she was in Paris, hiding after the release of a spicy, unauthorized biography of her life.

The registrar behind the counter smiled cordially.

"I'm here to see Mr. Delmont," Jenny said, taking the affirmative approach. "Unfortunately, I've left behind the number of his suite."

"Mr. Delmont?"

"Eric Delmont. He has an apartment here."

The man stared blankly at her from behind the counter. "I'm sorry, but we have no such person staying at our hotel."

"Could you check your records? I'm certain he said to meet him here." She knew full well there was no need for him to refer to the guest list. He was paid well for knowing who stayed in each room.

"I'm sorry, but I'm quite positive. Perhaps you should contact Mr. Delmont by telephone."

He was not being rude; he wasn't even being evasive. He was, in fact, completely professional. There was no way of determining from his manner whether Eric actually resided in the Pierre, or if the registrar was simply protecting his patron's privacy. No doubt there would have been word left at the desk if Eric had been expecting anyone to visit him. Jenny knew this as well as the man at the desk did. But it had been worth the try.

She turned away from the counter and walked toward the door leading to the street. Turning her head slightly, she noticed that the man she had just spoken to was now preoccupied with a middle-aged couple who had just arrived, judging by the suitcases being brought in by bellboys.

The last thing she wanted was to be thrown out of the hotel by the management which might view her as some kind of troublemaker. She'd have to be careful. Nearby, she noticed, was the gift shop, and Jenny walked in, pretending to shop for toiletries while she looked into the lobby through the glass wall.

The man behind the desk was no longer there; another had replaced him.

Leaving the gift shop a moment or two later, she strode quickly through the lobby, trying to blend in with other patrons headed for the bank of elevators on the far side. At the row of elevators, she pushed a button calling a car to the ground floor and waited, trying hard to appear nonchalant.

At last the car arrived, opening its doors and expelling a full load of passengers. She stepped aside, allowing the last person to disembark, then quickly entered and pushed the button to the top floor.

One by one, the other riders exited on their respective floors. She was left alone to ride to the eighth floor with only one other person.

The elevator bounced slightly and came to a stop. She had reached the top floor of the Pierre, the floor most likely to house its most distinguished visitors; it was the floor on which Eric might reside.

The man with her smiled and permitted her to step into the hall first. He followed, passing her at a brisk pace as she pretended to walk to a specific destination.

But there was something wrong. All the doors were marked by room numbers, and the rooms were spaced fairly close together—too close to belong to private apartments. Then she realized what the problem was. This wasn't the top floor of the Pierre at all. She remembered having counted the stories from the outside of the building as she approached. There had been eleven floors.

She back tracked to the elevators. There were five car doors on this floor, but when she had taken the ride up from the ground floor, there had been only four at street level. The fifth elevator was obviously a private car that led to the upper floors, off limits to anyone who did not live there.

Her theory was further substantiated by an examination of the button by its side. There was a special lock inside the button, which required a key.

The man had reached his room at the far end of the hall. She heard his keys rattle in a lock and turned to look. He was staring at her suspiciously.

"Need any help?" he called.

"No . . . thanks. I just realized I got off at the wrong floor."

"I see," he said, pausing for a second or two as if considering something. Then he stepped inside his room and shut the door.

She'd have to do something fast. It was entirely possible that the man would call downstairs to the management and suggest they keep an eye on the young woman loitering in the hallway on the eighth floor.

It was an absurd situation. She was actually starting to feel like a criminal—she, Jenny Gordon, the most honest of all people.

There was no use thinking she'd be able to take the elevator up; that was obviously impossible without a key in her possession.

That left the stairs as her only alternative.

The door marked "exit" at the end of the long hall opened onto a stairwell. Like the four elevators, from ground level, she found it, too, stopped at the eighth floor.

Feeling decidedly frustrated, Jenny returned to the other end of the hall. Here was another door, but unmarked. It was locked. She knew where it had to lead. Up.

Farther down from where she stood, a door opened and she jumped, expecting and fearing to see the man she had spoken to earlier emerge into the hall.

Instead, she watched a young maid wheel a cleaning cart from out of a room. She was coming Jenny's way, pushing the cart in front of her and humming softly to herself.

Jenny approached the girl. She opened her purse, appearing to be checking for something inside. As she passed the hotel maid, she smiled and continued to walk casually toward the elevators. Moving her hand to the elevator call button, she bypassed it and punched the wall instead, then pretended to wait for the car to arrive.

The maid had rolled her cart to the end of the hall to the unmarked door. She fumbled inside her pocket, brought out a large key ring and, whistling lightly to herself, opened the locked entrance. From the bottom shelf of her cleaning cart, she removed a large basket containing rags and what appeared to be cleaning compounds and fluids, before proceeding through the private door.

Jenny reacted at once. The door was half-open. Rapidly she moved down the hall, trying not to appear rushed and thus arouse suspicion.

The girl sensed someone behind her and looked out past the door.

"Darn!" Jenny said, managing to squeeze through the door just as the maid was pulling it closed. "I left my wallet upstairs in another purse."

Although not airtight, the explanation seemed to satisfy the young maid, and she continued up the stairs on her way to the ninth floor. Jenny followed closely behind.

She had feared that the entrance to the upper floors might also be locked and require a key, just as the private door off the eighth floor had. When the maid opened the door leading to the next floor's hall, Jenny was relieved to discover a key wasn't necessary. She'd be able to move up the stairwell and obtain entrance to the other floors on her own.

She entered the hall after the maid, who lugged along the large basket of cleaning supplies.

The ninth floor was carpeted in luxurious blue pile. Here, unlike the eighth floor, the walls were of Brazilian rosewood panels, joined at the seams by thin strips of polished brass. Oil paintings lined the walls and crystal chandeliers hung at intervals, lighting the passage with brilliant white lights that danced against the brass strips.

Jenny looked around her in awe. She had made it into the private haven of the powerful, and, more relevant to her present situation, the discreet. For there were no names on the doors to tell her which one might be Eric Delmont's.

"By the way," she said to the maid, trying to sound non-chalant, "you wouldn't know if Eric Delmont's returned from his trip to Germany, would you?"

She held her breath as the girl turned toward her. "Eric Delmont?" She looked at Jenny with a quizzical expression.

"Yes," Jenny rushed, nervous that the maid would catch on to her ploy and report her as a trespasser. "You do Mr Delmont's quarters, don't you?"

"Not me. I've got enough to do taking care of three apartments on this floor."

So Eric was in the Pierre. The maid hadn't denied his occupancy. All Jenny needed to know now was where in the hotel he was. "Oh, of course!" Jenny exclaimed dramatically. "For a moment I forgot you just do this floor."

The maid nodded and looked at her curiously. "Marie's the one who does the eleventh. She'd know what's going on with the people up there. But why don't you just call him yourself?" she asked, somewhat suspiciously, Jenny thought.

"Yes . . . I will. I'll do that," she stammered. "As soon as I get into my apartment." She started to back away. Her mind was racing in a million different directions. Eric was here and he was on the eleventh floor. The thought that she was this close to him, to the place where he lived, filled her with a sense of delight and an equal sense of panic.

He would have to realize how desperate she was to have gone to such elaborate measures to track him down. And what would she find when she got there? Somehow, dropping in on Eric unannounced didn't seem like such a good idea anymore. But she had come this far—she couldn't back down now.

The maid rapped gently against a door, waiting for the

resident to answer. Jenny walked briskly, purposefully down the hall, making it a point to jingle her keys. She prayed that someone would let the maid in soon, before it became obvious that she didn't belong on the ninth floor—or, for that matter, anywhere else in the Pierre.

To her great relief Jenny hear a click behind her and the voice of a woman greeting the maid; then the door shut on both of them.

The hall was clear.

Without wasting a moment, she dashed back to the stairs. Her heart pounded as she climbed to the tenth floor and bypassed it to continue on to the eleventh. At last! Triumphantly she entered the hallway at the top of the Pierre.

It was a hall unlike any she had ever seen or imagined. Rather than being long and narrow like traditional halls, this one was relatively small, and square in shape. It was lined entirely in white marble. Marble floors gave way to marble walls, and in the center of the room stood an ancient Roman statue of a beautiful woman.

Two doors faced each other at opposite sides of the hall, and she presumed these led to the apartments. But there was another, smaller door opposite where she stood and it took Jenny a moment or two to realize that this was the elevator, barely recognizable in its present form. A craftsman had camouflaged its identity by covering it with a screen that duplicated the look of the marble.

The two main doors were oversized arches, exact replicas of each other; and, unless she was mistaken, they were authentic Sythian portals, their faces hammered into intricate designs of leopards and mythical creatures sacred to the ancient civilization. Every inch of both doors had been covered in gold leaf.

The nerve that had propelled her thus far suddenly

dissolved. It was sheer madness to think she could appear at Eric's doorstep unannounced—especially when the doorstep was as intimidating as the one before which she now stood.

Timidly she had approached one of the doors to examine its detailed work. Then she turned and hurried back to the stairs, her heels against the marble echoing harshly in the tomblike quiet.

Before she could reach the door to the exit, a man's voice sounded behind her. Guiltily she reeled around and discovered a dignified man wearing a formal butler's uniform eyeing her disdainfully from one of the arches, now open.

"I think you had better explain yourself," he said stiffly.

Jenny did her best to look insulted. But her position was a weak one, and the man was scrutinizing her from beneath bushy white brows, waiting for her response.

"Well, you see, I was looking for someone and—"

"That someone's name?" he inquired, interrupting her brusquely.

"His name?" Visions of being marched through the Pierre's lobby, held on either arm by the hotel's management, an exhibition of ridicule to crowds of people, insinuated themselves in her mind as she stalled for time.

"Charles? Charles, let the lady in," commanded a female voice from beyond the open arch.

"Follow me," he said, motioning for Jenny to enter.

Jenny complied, puzzled that the voice she had heard from within the apartment sounded so familiar. As she entered a large living room she realized why. Before her, standing in front of an enormous painting done by Gainsborough, was none other than Candy McManus. Dressed in hot pink lounging pajamas and stroking a white

Persian cat, she looked at Jenny with a bemused expression in her dark brown eyes.

"I can imagine what you must be thinking," Jenny began, feeling like a complete fool.

"Thinking, Miss Gordon?" She furrowed her brow. "Lordy, my, I just don't know what to think. You see," she said, looking up toward the ceiling, "I was just sitting here petting kitty, when all of a sudden I looked up and what do you think I saw?"

Jenny followed the direction of Candy's gaze. A small television was installed high and flush against the wall, its tiny screen displaying a clear picture of the entire eleventh floor hall. Jenny blushed furiously, feeling more and more like a trespasser.

"I would assume," she said weakly, "that you saw me on that."

"Well, you're right. Absolutely. That's exactly what I saw. Much to my surprise, I might add."

"Look—"

Candy cut her off again. "Charles?" she called, and looked at Jenny. "Where is that man? I thought I'd get him to fix us something nice to eat and drink."

Jenny didn't know what to make of the woman from Texas.

"Candy, please," pleaded Jenny. "I'm not really in the mood for anything to eat or drink. I just came here to see Eric. I wanted to give him something. Something that he loaned me." The weight of the pendant felt heavy around her neck.

"Oh." Candy seemed disappointed. "Well, honey, Eric isn't here. But I am."

"Well, I can see that," replied Jenny, still unsure of what to make of her hostess.

"He isn't due back, either. Not for a while. That's why I've taken over his place. I promised him I'd look after all his beautiful things. They're just awfully beautiful, now, aren't they?"

Jenny flinched at the reference to beauty. Candy McManus might be guileless, but she was still a remarkably beautiful woman, and judging by the magnificent treasures assembled en masse in Eric's living room, he was an avid collector of all things beautiful. Even as Candy continued speaking, Jenny noticed a Ming vase of museum quality on the fireplace mantel.

"You know," Candy was saying, "it wasn't actually my very own idea to come here. It was daddy's. Now that's a fact," she added solemnly. "Daddy's in oil, you know. In Texas. Well, anyway," she went on, now smiling happily at Jenny, "Daddy wants me to have some culture besides all that silly money, so he just made me pack my bags and hightail it out here to soak up some European refinement."

"All very admirable, I'm sure," said Jenny politely, not the slightest bit interested. "Candy, do you have any idea where Eric is?"

Candy started to say something, then apparently thought better of it.

And once again, Jenny was forced to revise her opinion of Eric's stunning redheaded friend. She wasn't quite the empty-headed bauble she pretended to be, of that Jenny was certain. And it took considerable brains to play dumb. No, there was a lot more to Candy McManus than she allowed to show on the surface, and Jenny wondered why her hostess wanted her to think she was no more than a harmless ball of southern fluff.

"Jenny? I may call you Jenny, mayn't I?"

Jenny nodded her agreement.

"Well, Jenny, honey, you see I can't really help you. Eric said he had some important business to take care of and that's all I know. Now I surely do wish I could help you, but I just don't know a thing about what that boy's up to."

Whatever Eric was doing, one thing could be said for him; he picked his friends wisely. The viscount had covered for him. And now Candy. Two clams could have provided more information.

Jenny decided to give it one more try. "That vase," she said, "the one on the mantel—do you know where Eric got it?"

"Well, now, I'm not sure. I guess he brought it back from one of his trips."

"Business trips?" Jenny asked, fishing.

"Well," Candy said thoughtfully, "I don't rightly know what Eric does on his trips, but he's always bringing home the nicest things. He certainly does have good taste." Candy sighed and looked about the room as if overwhelmed by the furnishings. She walked to a small table and picked up a jade figurine. "You should have just seen the diamond bracelet he brought home from his last trip."

Jenny sucked in a small breath, waiting impatiently for Candy to continue.

"I could have just died when I saw it. I wanted it so much, you know. I told him I'd write him out a big fat check, right there on the spot. But, no, he went ahead and put it in his darned old safe." Candy pouted prettily and placed the figurine back on its oval rosewood stand.

"Maybe he'll bring you back something equally nice on his next trip," Jenny said, her mind racing from thought to thought.

"Maybe," Candy said, "but that bracelet he brought back from Marrakesh surely was nice."

Marrakesh.

So it *had* been Eric she had seen that night. Jenny felt as if she had been hit in the stomach.

"Are you all right?" Candy inquired solicitously, her face filled with concern. "You look funny."

"I feel more than funny," Jenny whispered. "I feel really, really awful."

"Was it something I said?" Candy called after her, as she walked rapidly from the room.

"No," Jenny returned, continuing to walk straight ahead, her vision blurred by tears. The mysterious Eric Delmont had suddenly become less of a mystery.

Chapter 6

Jenny was only too thankful that Mr. Farrar had sent her to Copenhagen to investigate the possibility of using a new hotel that had recently opened.

There was no use in her stewing over Eric. He obviously didn't want to call her, and as Anne had been quick to point out, it was probably for her own good. Everything she had discovered about Eric's activities was based on sheer coincidence and happenstance; but the evidence was piling up, and it wasn't in his favor.

One thing was clear. Eric had money, and a lot of it. How he got it, was the all-consuming question. She remembered the night at Chez Cary when she had asked him about his work and he had hedged, reluctant to divulge his occupation.

From her visit to his apartment, she knew that he traveled frequently and that he brought back expensive jewelry and objets d'art, such as the diamond bracelet and the Chinese vases. If he was a collector, or an art dealer, then why hadn't he just told her?

None of it made sense. Indeed, all of it pointed to something that was decidedly underhanded, and yet, try as she might, she couldn't stop believing in him.

It was the last week in January. Copenhagen was under seige by a swirling mass of snow. The wind howled dramatically, seeming to call out in multitudinous voices carried from the past, as it changed its timbre in accord with its flow through narrow cobbled streets, rushing over steeples and around lamp posts.

Jenny had checked into the hotel and had been given a thorough and gracious tour of the hotel's accommodations, which included several classes of lodgings. Mr. Farrar had been right to send her. The hotel was all that it had purported to be in its slick, colorful brochures, and its rates were lower than two of the other hotels they had previously used when booking tours in that city.

The manager had made reservations for her to dine that night in its restaurant, Andersen's—named, of course, for the famous Danish writer of fairy tales, Hans Christian Andersen.

Pushing Eric firmly from her mind, at least for the time being, Jenny took advantage of her good fortune to visit one of the world's most romantic cities.

The royal flag was flying over Amalienborg Palace, indicating that the queen was in residence. Braving the cold, keening wind, she toured the enormous open court of the palace. Members of the Danish Royal Guard were on duty, their towering black bearskin hats rapidly becoming cones of white fur as the snow continued to fall. They seemed the very embodiment of the little tin soldier in Andersen's fairy tale, their uniforms from a bygone era, their rifles at their sides.

Even during the winter Copenhagen was a magical city,

an environment designed for lovers. Despite her desire to forget Eric, the thought made Jenny ache inside, and she brushed away a tear that threatened to spill from the corner of her eye. He was as much a part of the past, never to be recovered, as were the guards in their anachronistic outfits, and the sooner she could accept that fact, the better off she would be.

When she returned to the hotel, the lobby buzzed with activity. A sign was posted, welcoming the International Philatelic Congress. Not having the slightest idea of what that was, she asked, and was informed by a young man wearing thick bifocals that it was a gathering of stamp collectors from all over the world.

Respectable-looking men in dark suits and no-nonsense ties mingled together in small groups as they waited for the doors to the banquet room to open. Most carried one or two briefcases with them. A few had opened albums containing neat rows of stamps covered by plastic, and with their heads bent over the contents, they exchanged muffled comments on their worth.

Jenny glanced at her watch and saw that there would be ample opportunity for her to return to her room, bathe and dress for dinner. A hot soak would be welcome after the afternoon she had spent in the chilled air.

Three elevators lined the far end of the lobby. Jenny punched the button at the side and was lost in thoughts of her family when the door in front of her finally opened and several hotel guests emerged, their voices raised in animated conversation.

A short, rotund man in an unflattering gray tweed suit, bounded from the elevator, an enormous briefcase swinging dangerously from his right arm. As he lifted his other arm to wave to someone in the lobby, he lost his balance and lurched clumsily against a woman who had just exited beside him. She, in turn, fell into Jenny.

"So sorry," the woman apologized, trying to right herself.

Jenny looked up, and stared in amazement at the face that greeted her. Candy McManus stared directly at her, her own brown eyes wide and showing equal amazement at Jenny's presence.

Jenny backed away from the elevator. Candy followed her reluctantly, appearing slightly ruffled by the unexpected encounter.

"Why, what a coincidence," Candy began, her voice light but her manner awkward in a way Jenny could never have imagined.

"Yes, isn't it?" replied Jenny airily, studying her companion covertly. Something was bothering Candy. She watched intently as the beautiful redhead darted a quick look over her shoulder as if searching for something—or someone. Definitely she was uneasy, yet determined to hide her discomfort behind a dazzling smile.

"Are you here on vacation?" Candy asked in a voice reserved for cocktail parties.

"Business," Jenny answered.

"Oh, how nice that you're able to travel," Candy said.

"And, you? What brings you to Copenhagen?"

"Me?"

"Yes, it's not the best time of year for seeing the sights, is it?" Jenny continued to study Candy carefully, at the same time managing to affect an outward air of complete unconcern.

"Why, I've come to see the culture, of course," Candy replied. She continued to smile, but it was increasingly obvious to Jenny that Candy was as ill at ease as she was herself.

"Ah, yes, I remember. Your father wanted you to have the grand tour. What have you seen so far?"

"Nothing. I just arrived. Today," Candy said haltingly.

Jenny had the unmistakable impression that even if Candy McManus had arrived two years ago, she'd still be at a loss to answer her last question. She didn't like to think of herself as an intellectual snob, but somehow the idea of Candy touring art galleries and museums seemed, if not ludicrous, at least highly unlikely.

And that left the unanswered question: what *was* Candy McManus doing in Copenhagen? *Really?*

Before she had the opportunity to find out, Candy cut short their conversation. Placing her hand lightly on Jenny's arm, she spoke as fast as Jenny had ever heard her speak before. "Hate to dash, but I do have to run now. Have to meet someone. Awfully nice to have seen you," she said, and before Jenny could reply, she had disappeared into the crowded room of milling stamp collectors.

RESERVATIONS FOR DINNER had been made for eight o'clock. The Andersen Room was charming, a vision of good taste and warm congeniality.

The manager of the hotel had ordered for her, sending as a main course the specialty of the house: roast goose, flaming under an orange brandy sauce.

It was ten-thirty by the time she had finished with the lavish dessert, but the manager had seen to the last touch. She was not allowed to leave without first sampling an after-dinner drink of chocolate mint liqueur, topped by whipped cream.

She sipped the drink slowly, enjoying the group of musicians who had assembled on a raised dais at the far end of the room, playing soft, romantic music for couples to dance to.

Many of the diners had left; their tables had been cleared, and clean cloths had replaced the used ones. The atmosphere had been subtly altered. A new crowd of people began to enter, taking seats around the dance floor and ordering beverages from the bar.

Jenny recognized many of the men seated at tables near her as belonging to the Philatelic Congress gathering.

A group of four people, three men and a woman, entered the restaurant and were shown to a table at the edge of the dance floor. As they moved through the room, Jenny gave a gasp of astonishment.

Two of the men were strangers to her, but she knew the woman and one of the men only too well. He was Eric Delmont, while she, dressed in a form-fitting strapless yellow evening gown and wearing a spray of diamonds flashing at her neck, was none other than Candy McManus. She walked at his side, clutching his arm possessively.

So that was the reason Candy had appeared nervous, Jenny thought. She hadn't wanted her to know that Eric was here.

What a fool she had been, believing that story Candy had told her about taking care of Eric's apartment while he was out of town. They had both probably had a good laugh over her visit to his apartment. No doubt Candy was rich, and no doubt Eric found that a very attractive asset.

But then, to be truthful, it was plain that Candy had other obvious attractions besides her father's money. She was a beautiful woman, and Jenny was quite sure now that she was also very clever.

Eric, looking debonair in a dark, pin-striped suit, had risen from his chair. Jenny watched as he pulled Candy's chair from the table, politely offering his arm to her as she rose.

They crossed the dance floor together, and Candy dropped her hand from his arm, seeking his hand and twining her fingers in his.

To Jenny, it was as if a whip had torn into her flesh, searing her with pain and humiliation. The feelings were further compounded as she watched the man who had once held her close move his hand langorously across another woman's back.

They were together, swaying in time to the music, and the sight filled Jenny with both envy and hatred; a strange hatred for the man who had made a complete fool of her, a hatred for the woman now dancing in his arms, and a hatred for herself for being so stupid.

For a month she had mooned over a man who probably had ten women fawning over him in every city in which he stopped to conduct his business— whatever *that* was.

She had just been one more conquest to add to his collection.

She had heard of men like Eric Delmont, men who fed upon the flattery of women, toying with their hearts and leaving them to lick their wounded egos when he tired of their admiring attention.

For the time being she had seen enough. For the time being—and forever. Quickly, angrily, she rose from her seat. In her desperation to be gone, she knocked against her table, sending her glass dessert bowl flying through the air to land with a resounding crash on the floor.

The sound of the glass as it shattered against the hard floor seemed deafening against the mellow music being played. Heads turned in her direction.

Humiliated beyond words, she blushed and bent to pick up the shards of glass before anyone was hurt.

A waiter hurried to her aid and she stepped back, allowing him to finish the job and spare her further embarrassment.

The music had stopped, and as people returned to their seats, Jenny collected her purse and shawl. She was about to leave the room when the two men who had come in with Eric and Candy passed her.

To her horror, she discovered that Candy and Eric were only steps behind.

It was too late to turn. Her path crossed theirs exactly at the door. It was a moment from a nightmare. Nothing, nothing could have been more awkward, embarrassing and guaranteed to hurt.

She could smell the faint aroma of Eric's cologne, the same scent that he had worn for her, and the same sensation of sweet happiness and desire flooded through her as it had when they had first met in the drawing room of Château des Fleurs.

What happened next took only a second, but to Jenny it seemed like an eternity that would hurt her forever.

There was no way that she could have avoided him. Eric was directly beside her as she began to pass through the door. Their shoulders touched, and he moved away slightly, politely.

Looking down at her, his eyes were cold and distant. There was no sign of recognition. Her peripheral vision took in Candy's face. There, too, there was no emotion, no sign that they had ever spoken, nor even met.

"Pardon me," Eric said mildly, as if to a stranger, and walked on.

"It's all right . . ." Jenny murmured, her words trailing off as she stared after him miserably.

It was as if he had never been with her. Suddenly

frightened, she clutched the pendant still around her neck,
reminder of another time and place that she now doubted
ever existed.

Her room was a welcome retreat. Sinking down onto her
bed, she stared at the ceiling, tracing the shadows with
eyes that burned with tears that would not come.

She had loved Eric, hopelessly, romantically, and all in
vain—that much was obvious. But there was something
else that troubled her. She began to question her own judgment, the same sound reasoning capabilities that had served
her in good stead thus far in her life. How could she have
been so wrong in this case? How could she have been so
wrong about Eric? And why would he have given her a
valuable necklace if she'd meant so little to him?

For the next hour she lay on her bed, her mind working
to put together the pieces of an intricate mental jigsaw puzzle, going over everything she could remember about her
relationship with Eric, from the moment they had first
met, to the bewildering encounter in the restaurant that
evening.

Nothing made sense. Without bothering to undress, she
closed her eyes, willing the tension to drain from her body
and allow her to sleep. It was no use. Her mind seemed
to be working like a spinning wheel, going round and
round . . . endlessly. Faces appeared, snatches of conversations she'd had with Candy played again through her
mind, the vision of a vase in Eric's Paris apartment; all
these ghostly images tumbled through her mind, taunting
her, challenging her to put them in their proper places.

Struck by a thought, she suddenly sat up on the bed. She
remembered something from earlier in the evening. Candy
had used the elevator to enter the hotel lobby. That meant

she must be registered in the hotel. Jenny rose from the bed, her mind forming a plan as she dashed cold water from the bathroom tap over her face.

Candy McManus would be a very good person to visit. And this time, Jenny vowed, she was going to get some answers—from one of them. This time they would talk.

A quick check downstairs at the desk gave her the information she wanted. In a way, Jenny was surprised. It would have been more in keeping if Candy had registered under a different name, or had given instructions to the hotel not to disclose her occupancy.

But in this case Jenny had an advantage. She had specifically asked the hotel manager if she could examine their registration procedures to include as part of her report on his hotel. Although it had undoubtedly seemed an odd request for the time of night, he had complied and she now had the information that would take her to Candy McManus. She had also learned that Eric was not registered at the same hotel.

Several minutes later, Jenny tapped lightly against Candy's door. The room was quiet within. Jenny knocked again. A moment later, she heard the sound of someone walking to the door, then a low, female voice.

"Yes?"

"Candy, it's me. Jennifer Gordon. I need to speak with you." Jenny waited.

"Jennifer?" The voice sounded alarmed.

Jenny could guess why. It wasn't pleasant for a person to be trapped in their own deceptions. Now Candy would have to face her and tell her why she had ignored her in the restaurant, and why Eric had pretended not to know her.

"Jenny, go away. Go away." Candy's voice behind the door was quiet, rushed, almost desperate.

"No," said Jenny firmly. "I'm not leaving until we speak."

There was the sound of a lock being turned, and the door opened.

Candy was dressed in the strapless yellow evening gown, still wearing the diamonds. Her manner was nervous, furtive. She glanced quickly over Jenny's shoulder, as if expecting someone to be there.

"Look, Jenny, this really isn't a good time to talk." She started to close the door, but Jenny put out her hand to keep it open.

"I think it is. I think this is as good a time to talk as any other. And I want some answers."

Candy glared at her. "Look, I don't mean to be rude, but you *must* get away from here. Now."

There was none of the sugar in her voice this time. It was hard and sharp, with only the hint of her Southern accent to remind Jenny that this was the same woman speaking who had drawled her way through an entire visit in Eric's apartment.

"No." Jenny was adamant. She was tired of being in the dark. If Candy and Eric had a relationship going, then fine. It might hurt—no, she corrected, it *would* most definitely hurt—to learn for certain what she already suspected. But, at least she'd have her self-respect back.

Candy sighed and stepped away from the door. She motioned for Jenny to follow and closed the door after them. Both women stood just inside the room facing each other warily.

"You knew where Eric was the last time I saw you in Paris," Jenny accused. "Why did you feign ignorance? What good does all this charade do you—and Eric?"

Candy was silent. At that moment Jenny realized

something she wouldn't have expected from Candy McManus. The beautiful redhead was frightened. Her face was pale and her hands trembled.

"Candy . . . what's wrong? Tell me," Jenny urged.

"I can't," she whispered. "Now, look—" her voice was tough again "—you must leave this room. Leave it now. I can't give you any information about Eric. I *can't*. Do you understand?"

Jenny searched the woman's face. For once, she believed Candy. Anyone who looked that scared had to be telling the truth.

"Okay, but—"

She didn't have time to finish. Candy had opened the door leading into the hallway.

"Get out," she said hurriedly. Her voice was soft, but lethal.

Jenny moved from the room. Just before the door closed after her, Candy spoke. "Jenny . . . it's for your own good." Her voice wasn't particularly kind. She was just stating a fact.

The door closed. Jenny heard the security latch move into place, then the shrill sound of the telephone as it rang in Candy's room.

On the third ring, Jenny heard Candy answer.

"Yes?" Candy's accent was thick again. "It's all right now," she said, the accent now diminished. "Yes, it's clear."

The receiver was returned to the hook with a faint click. Jenny heard Candy move through her room.

Quickly she moved away from the door and walked rapidly to the elevator at the end of the hall. Candy had been wrong about one thing she had said—things weren't clear. She, at least, didn't understand *what* was going on.

Chapter 7

Jenny had been exhausted when she'd returned home from Denmark. She had kissed everyone hello, given Allan and Michael their gifts she had purchased for them at the airport, assured her mother she was fine, and had then fallen soundly asleep from six in the evening until the following morning at eleven o'clock.

When she awoke, she found Michael sprawled on his stomach in the living room, the television blaring, and an army of two-inch-high soldiers engaged in furious battle with Michael as their commander-in-chief.

"Jenny!" he crowed delightedly, as soon as he saw her. "I got to stay home!"

Jenny laughed and nodded. She didn't need to be told why, either. It happened on more than one occasion in the past when she had been gone a few days. Michael feigned the beginnings of a cold, believing his acting ability convinced one and all that he should stay home and recuperate. Of course he convinced no one, but he was so adorable, so utterly lovable, it was almost impossible to resist his charm.

Jenny found a note from her mother on the kitchen table.

"I've called Mr. Farrar," she read. "Told him I insisted you stay home and get some rest. Will be back soon. Went to get meat for dinner."

"I'm not really sick," Michael confessed, as he watched her pour orange juice into a glass.

"Really? You look sick," Jenny said solemnly.

"I do?"

"No . . . not really."

"Phew," he sighed. "I really wanted to be with you. You're hardly ever home anymore."

He followed her into the living room. Jenny sat down on the couch, drinking the juice and leafing through a new fashion magazine. Michael continued to chatter while the television droned on in the background, a dour-faced newsman reading a report.

"Jen . . . look. These guys are going to wipe out these other guys. They're the bad ones. Jenny . . . look. . . ." Michael pleaded, but to no avail.

Jenny had suddenly become absorbed in what the newsman was saying.

"At the International Philatelic Congress in Copenhagen, it was discovered yesterday that two stamp collections were stolen, valued at one hundred and fifty thousand crowns."

"Jenny, you aren't—"

"Michael, please," she interrupted sharply, rising to turn up the sound on the television set.

The newsman continued his report. "The first victim was a participant from Germany. He discovered toward noon that one of his albums, worth forty thousand crowns, had disappeared. A few hours later, a participant from Spain found out he, also, had been robbed. His album contained some very old and rare stamps that are valued at around one hundred and ten thousand crowns. The police do not suspect any of the participants. It is thought the thefts were committed by one or more seasoned international thieves."

The newsman rifled through some papers on his stand, raised his head and looked into the camera. "Also on the international crime scene, Candy McManus, socialite daughter of Texas oil tycoon, Ruford T. McManus, reports being robbed of jewels from her Copenhagen hotel suite. The robbery occurred during the same time period as the other stamp thefts. Miss McManus stated that it was no secret that she was in the city. Her picture had appeared in several society columns along with articles stating her plans to visit Copenhagen. . . . Meanwhile, in Iceland, environmentalists—"

Jenny flicked off the television set.

Michael watched as she paced the floor, stepping carefully over his tiny battlefield.

"Is there something wrong?" he wanted to know, his face screwed into a puzzled expression.

"No, not anymore." She would forget all about Eric Delmont. She would study her art. She would work at the travel agency. And she'd make a concerted effort to find someone else that interested her—although her heart, quite literally, wasn't in it.

When her mother returned home from shopping, Jenny kissed Michael goodbye, explaining that she had to drop her travel report off to Mr. Farrar before her Wednesday night art class.

The bus rumbled through the midafternoon Paris traffic, drowning out the sounds of lesser vehicles beside it. The conversations of people around her were faint and soothing, and soon her mind drifted to subjects she had recently declared off limits.

Candy McManus had been robbed. If Eric had been involved in the thefts, then Candy would surely have known about them. She was smart and deceptive—not a woman easily taken advantage of by anyone, not even by Eric Delmont, Jenny wagered. That Candy herself had been robbed just didn't make sense.

The bus came to a fast stop and the man sitting beside her stood and pushed past her. At the last minute she realized that it was her stop and jumped from her seat, making it out the exit just as the door closed behind her.

Jenny walked into the agency to find Monica and Mr. Farrar engaged in a heated discussion over a customer's complaint of an itinerary that Monica had contrived. Apparently, it had barely permitted the woman time to eat and sleep before she was off to another country.

"Well, if she wasn't so fat," Jenny heard Monica say, "she could probably move faster."

Mr. Farrar frowned at Monica's remark, deciding obviously that angry words could not make good an unfortunate situation.

He looked away from Monica and smiled broadly at Jenny when she came in. Crooking his finger for her to join him, he marched into his private office.

"So," he said, putting his feet on top of his desk and leaning back into his chair, "how did you enjoy Copenhagen?"

"It was lovely," Jenny said, handing him the written report of the hotel's accommodations.

"Thanks." He opened the manila envelope and casually

perused her remarks. "Heard there was a little trouble there," he said, looking over the papers.

"The thefts, you mean." Would she never be free of the subject of Eric Delmont? Not that Mr. Farrar would have any inkling he even existed, or that the subject was such a sore one. But to her, it was just one more unwelcome opportunity for the image of Eric to rise into her consciousness. And that she could well do without.

"We've got to be careful we don't involve our customers in anything like that."

Jenny winced. If he only knew how involved she was with the man who could very well be responsible for the crimes he wished to avoid exposing their clients to. . . . "I'm sure the hotel in Copenhagen isn't to blame," she murmured. "You'll see from my report that it's an excellent establishment."

"Yes, yes," Mr. Farrar said, and tossed the report on his desk. "Tell me, how would you like to continue traveling for me? My wife's complained for years that I'm gone too much. I can trust you, Jenny. You do a good job and you know how to handle yourself with people. I like that. It leaves a good impression of our operation."

Jenny was flattered. "I'd love to travel, of course."

In fact, she'd like to get as far away from Eric Delmont as possible. And she'd like to keep as busy as possible. That, too, would help her forget.

But then she thought of Monica. Dependent, frequently irritable, yet incorrigible Monica, sitting there day after day, slumped over her desk, painstakingly working out the details of other people's dreams, their trips to Tahiti, their junkets to the Greek Islands, their romantic sojourns in Italy . . . .

"Mr. Farrar," she began, "you know, of course, that I love the opportunity to travel. I'd always hoped I'd be able to take trips when I took the job with you, and it's been like, well, like a dream come true."

"But?" he prompted.

"Yes . . . but. I was wondering whether it might not be more fair to have Monica go on a trip once in a while."

Mr. Farrar's face colored a bright red. "What? Monica! That . . . that annoyance out there! You can't be serious. We'd lose all our business."

Jenny couldn't help but smile at the thought of Monica insulting everyone she met.

"But perhaps it might do something to sweeten her disposition if she got to go somewhere. It's awfully glamorous being able to travel. And, well, Monica doesn't seem to have much to look forward to in life."

"That's her problem," he barked. "I'm not a fairy godfather here. I run a business." He shuffled through some papers on his desk, the cue for Jenny to leave. Well, at least she'd tried.

She returned to the outer office to find Monica on the telephone, her face pained and disagreeable as she wrote down notes from a customer.

Jenny straightened her desk and made a quick call to Anne, asking her to meet her after her art class at a café they both knew.

Monica slammed down the telephone. "The rich!" she snorted contemptuously. "They think they own the whole, lousy world!"

"They might," Jenny quipped, gathering her coat and putting on her hat and gloves.

Monica simmered down. "So, how was the world? Speaking of such things."

"The world is just fine," Jenny replied, "and how was aris while I was gone?"

"The same as usual. Dull. Why is it that all the travel brochures describe Paris as such a romantic city? Anywhere less romantic would be hard to find."

"Yes, I know what you mean," Jenny said wistfully, and the sadness in her voice was evident, even to her.

Something in Monica's manner suddenly made Jenny take notice. She seemed agitated about something, as if she wanted to say something but couldn't.

"Is something wrong?" Jenny asked.

"Wrong?" echoed Monica. "Of course something's wrong. Something is always wrong with me." She paused, then asked ruefully, "Isn't that what you expect to hear?"

"Maybe," Jenny conceded, "but somehow I think this is different. Is there something specific bothering you? Look, if you need to talk, all you have to do is tell me."

Monica didn't respond. Not verbally, anyway. But her hand tapped nervously on her desk and her face was flushed.

"Well, I'm off then," Jenny announced finally tired of waiting for Monica to make up her mind. She could feel her co-worker's eyes following her out the door. Whatever was bothering Monica, she'd just have to wait until Monica was ready to share it with her.

JENNY'S ART CLASS had gone well. Her professor liked her; he said she had talent. That had lifted her spirits. A little anyway.

When she arrived at the café, Anne was already waiting for her.

"Hi! Tell me all about beautiful Copenhagen. It's somewhere I've always wanted to go," Anne said enthusiastically. "That is," she said in a low voice, confidential voice, "Monsieur le Vicomte and I are very interested in seeing a great deal of the world together."

"Hmm," Jenny said, unbuttoning her coat. "This sounds like an item."

"Item? Item? This is most definitely an item," Anne said, leaning over the table and almost spilling the hot chocolate she had been sipping. "This is the real thing."

"That has a familiar ring to it."

"Jen," Anne said, reaching over and squeezing Jenny's hand, "Quentin is *magnifique*! He's all my dreams come true, for real."

"He's rich," stated Jenny, matter-of-factly.

"No . . . that is, not exactly. About a hundred years ago, his family was rich, but unfortunately they lost it all in some war."

"Ah, yes," Jenny said, flagging down a waiter, "impoverished royalty."

She ordered a cup of expresso and turned her attention back to Anne, "Well, then, if the viscount is not rich, he must be very handsome indeed." Jenny raised her eyebrows up and down.

Anne made a forlorn face and shook her head. "Negative, my friend. Quentin is neither handsome, nor tall."

"This really does sound serious," Jenny said, amusement dancing in her eyes.

"I'll tell you just how serious it is. Quentin is average-looking. To be truthful, you might say that he's bordering on mousey. And, if he doesn't take special care, he's in constant danger of getting lost in crowds, he's so short."

"But—"

Anne interrupted, "But he's good and kind and fascinating and witty, and—"

"You love him," Jenny laughed, feeling good for her friend.

"How'd you guess?"

"Psychic powers."

"What about you?" Anne said, after they had discussed the incomparable and multitudinous merits of one Quentin Duval.

Jenny turned her head away, pretending to be absorbed in the other patrons seated around the restaurant.

"Oh, I get it. You haven't heard a word from Eric Delmont yet." Anne gave Jenny a knowledgeable, I-told-you-so look.

"I saw him."

"Well then? Why the long face?"

It was painful in the extreme, but Jenny related the entire incident of Eric's complete rejection at the restaurant in Copenhagen. She told Anne about the stamp thefts, about Candy McManus, and about Candy's jewels also being stolen.

When she had finished, Anne had only one piece of advice. "Forget him," she said emphatically.

"I will."

"No, you won't. I know you, Jenny Gordon. You're stubborn. You should forget him, but you're going to think about him and worry about him, and you're going to get yourself into one big mess. Mark my words."

"Anne, it's over," she insisted, then laughed at herself. What did she mean, over? It had never begun, not for Eric, anyway.

Anne stared at her for a moment, an expression of intense concentration on her face. "All right," she announced finally, and rather too loudly, Jenny thought. "I've got it all worked out. I'm going to get someone who'll be perfect for you. I'll talk to Quentin about it tomorrow. Don't you worry about a thing—it's out of your hands and into Quentin's."

Jenny only wished it *were* possible to forget about everything, to be able to put her feelings into someone else's care.

Chapter 8

Six months later Jenny found herself in Madrid, regretting that she hadn't taken the subway. Mr. Farrar had warned her about the heat when he'd made the plans for her to visit the city in August. Next time she'd listen to him.

It was the day of the last bullfight of the season, and Calle de Alcala, one of the city's main boulevards, was thronged with tourists like herself, eager to see the pageantry that was part of Spain's colorful history.

She, however, was not exactly eager to attend what she had told Mr. Farrar she considered a barbaric and cruel custom. Nevertheless, it was part of her job to report on current attractions, so that the agency's customers were assured of the best travel arrangements.

For seven months now, she had traveled extensively throughout Europe for Mr. Farrar, finding each trip enjoyable.

Anne had done her best to make her forget Eric Delmont, and to a large extent she had succeeded. Quentin had introduced her to several attractive men. Had she not been so busy with art school and her job, she might have become more involved with a rather charming medical doctor Quentin and Anne had introduced her to at a party.

The man had been attentive and considerate—perhaps not dashing, like Eric—but certainly someone deserving of her affection. But the feeling just wasn't there—the complete abandon that had enveloped her when she had been with Eric. The delicious tingling sensations she had felt in his presence. No, the man could not replace Eric.

But time had helped to heal much of the raw ache she felt when his image appeared in her mind. She had got over her rejection, and the feeling of despair had been replaced by another emotion. Should she ever see Eric again, she would speak to him rationally and objectively, returning the necklace to him with a prepared speech. Only then would she be able to shut him out of her life forever.

It was this that she dreamed about, being able to regain her own self-respect. The necklace, which she still wore around her neck, served as a reminder to her to be ready when the day came that she would once again run into Eric face-to-face. For some reason Anne and Quentin refused to believe her rationale. Well, she thought, as she walked along the wide boulevard, in the end she would show them.

Half of the arena was still bathed in sunshine when she entered at five o'clock. The other part was mercifully cooler, late-afternoon shadows casting a veil over spectators waiting for the spectacle to begin.

Musicians played the first phrases of a *paso-doble*, announcing the parade was about to start. At once two men on horses entered and circled the arena, their expressions of haughty arrogance accentuating their positions as being enviable, removed from the scope of the commonplace man.

A wave of excitement radiated through the crowds in response to the horns. The matadors had arrived. The men entered, graceful and slim in their ornate costumes that glittered under the dying sun like bursts of fire when the sequins caught the light. Elegant, disdainful, they paraded before the masses in the stands.

Whatever she thought of the cruelty, Jenny had to admit the excitement generated by the theatrical environment was contagious. She craned her neck to watch the celebration of primitive bravery form in the ring below.

The banderilleros came after the matadors; then two picadors riding horses with right eyes carefully blindfolded. Players of lesser importance followed, and finally mules, covered with hundreds of bells and colored ribbons, paraded through the arena.

Minutes later a magnificent creature, an ebony black bull full of pent-up energy charged into the ring with flaring nostrils, the dust billowing around him as he thundered across the arena. Jenny averted her eyes. No longer was the scene below to her liking.

The crowd roared. The matador was obviously putting on quite a show. Jenny looked around her, focusing her attention elsewhere than on the activity in the ring. Her eyes traveled over the spectators.

It was not difficult to identify the tourists from the locals. Jenny wondered what others thought of her. Did they place her as being an American, or was she clearly a Frenchwoman? Perhaps neither was correct. In some ways the world was shrinking, and the styles people wore served to diminish any obvious differences in culture.

Several rows down an old woman, her face creased into a landscape of loose wrinkles, stood and shouted energetically for the matador to put an end to the bull.

Next to her sat a younger woman, her profile boasting a small, turned-up nose; her hair was long and blond. She looked like many of the beautiful women that graced the beaches on the Riviera. The contrast between the wizened old woman and the young woman in the bright pink sun dress was remarkable. Jenny lifted her camera, bringing it to her eye to capture the incongruity.

It was him.

There was no mistake. Through the lens of her camera, the face was blurred, but even before she adjusted the clarity and brought the strong, familiar profile into focus, she was certain.

Eric Delmont sat twenty rows in front of her. The blond woman was his companion, obviously, for he had moved his arm to her shoulder.

This was the moment she had waited for, and yet now that it was here, Jenny was frightened. She wasn't sure of her emotions. The sight of him, so close, so handsome, so familiar to her from the hundreds of dreams, brought back emotions she had thought—had prayed—were buried.

No. She would collect herself. This time she would deal with him on her own terms. If she were to be discarded, then at least she would have the satisfaction of walking away on her own two feet, her head held high.

There was no chance to reach him now. Too many people separated them, and whatever she had to say to him would have been lost in the noise. She would wait for him to leave after the bullfight, perhaps allowing him one more chance to recognize her, as he had been unwilling to do in Copenhagen. The anger she'd built up against him over the past few months gave her an advantage. She was cooler this time, no longer the quivering young woman with the broken heart.

The performance ended and the crowds pushed toward the exits, raucously appraising each matador for bravery, for style, for handsomeness.

Jenny kept her eyes on the couple who had just risen and were slowly moving toward her. The blond woman was animated, turning her head quickly to take in whatever sights were available to her. The man smiled down at her, amused, but not participating in her excitement.

He was detached, Jenny thought, just as he had appeared the night she had met him at Château des Fleurs. Detached, that is, until he decided to turn on the charm that he knew how to use so well. Eric Delmont was a manipulator par excellence. Jenny found it curious that she wasn't even jealous of the woman at his side. She was beginning to doubt that Eric could care for anyone genuinely.

They were nearer to her now, still moving slowly, but it was necessary for her to begin to file out of the row she was in, or miss the chance of joining them as they walked up the steps to the exit.

She timed it exactly and moved into place just at the right moment. The blonde was between them. Eric had not noticed her presence beside them yet. Jenny decided to walk a bit farther without alerting his attention. It would be interesting to hear a little of their conversation, and besides, it would give her more time to steel herself for the moment when their eyes met.

They were on the platform outside the exit. In a minute they would turn, possibly disappear. It had to be now—or never.

"Eric!"

The blond woman turned to her first. Her expression was one of puzzlement, and she looked up at her companion. He smiled faintly and looked back at Jenny.

"Eric. I have something to give you." Her hand reached up for the pendant around her neck. His eyes followed. There was a glimmer of recognition as his attention was drawn to the necklace. He motioned to the girl with him to wait.

Jenny backed away from the main throng, finding a place against the wall to speak.

His eyes looked into hers, blue and probing, yet he didn't speak.

She drew in a long breath, blinked to keep her eyes clear and steady, then began. "It's wonderful to see you, Eric," she said quietly. "It's been such a long time."

He remained completely silent. Jenny trembled and fought to control her emotions. She could feel herself getting angry. Even now he barely acknowledged their acquaintance, and he certainly did not appear remorseful. He didn't even have the courtesy to pretend that he had meant to call her, to beg her understanding. Anything. The man was a cold, unfeeling, conceited . . . Greek god. As she stared up at his incredibly handsome face, she found it hard to believe that anyone could have such a ruthless disregard for another person's feelings. She had meant merely to hand the necklace to him, along with a short and dignified speech, walk away, and have done with him forever. But now she couldn't—wouldn't. She'd make him wait for the necklace. She'd test just how cool he was, because if he wanted his pendant back, then it was going to be on her terms.

"Look," she continued, before he could offer some excuse as to why he had to leave, once again making her look foolish, "I've got to go now, but I've wanted to give you back the necklace for a long time."

His eyes seemed to be devouring the stone within the silver setting.

"Anyway," she went on, "I wouldn't dream of handing it back to you without having it properly cleaned first." She stopped for a second, as if thinking. "I know, I've got tonight free. Meet me at six o'clock for dinner." She kept her eyes steady, realizing how brazen her invitation must seem.

But Eric only smiled. It was not an unpleasant smile, but somehow secretive and somewhat condescending. The warmth that had once attracted her to him was completely gone. And of that she was glad. Because now she could be free of his charm, free of him. Just as soon as she gave him back the necklace.

Bowing low, he took her hand in his and brought it to his lips, brushing his mouth lightly over her fingers, a mocking, courtly gesture. "At six, then. Tonight at El Cordoba."

Instantly he was gone.

Jenny stood against the wall, her heart beating wildly. The nerve! Did he think he was so irresistible he could sweep her off her feet with his pretentious, old-world gestures?

Well, she thought angrily, if he wanted to play games, so could she. Just this one last time. There was no time to waste. She'd go straight back to the hotel and prepare herself, for this was one night she wanted to look her best. It would be a night for them both to remember.

ERIC WAS ALREADY SEATED in the cocktail lounge of the El Cordoba when she arrived. It would not have been out of character for him to have let her wait, and she was glad that at least she had been spared that indignity.

When he saw her he rose immediately and joined her in the lobby. The maitre d' appeared at their side as if by magic. He bowed his head in greeting, speaking to Eric in rapid Spanish, the tone of his voice deferential, his manner unctuous. Eric returned in fluent Spanish what Jenny assumed were pleasantries. She had to admit he was a man of many talents. And of many surprises.

The restaurant Eric had chosen was on par with the Chez Cary—elegant and understated. But how very different were the emotions that had brought her to meet him this night! She could not pretend he didn't attract her even now, for he was undoubtedly one of the best-looking men she had ever seen.

Tonight, however, she detected in him a coldness, an icy reserve, that wasn't entirely attractive, and she wondered if love had previously blinded her to it.

"You're looking lovely this evening," Eric began, looking not at her, but at the wine list the waiter had brought him.

"Thank you." Jenny was looking her best, and knew it. Her hair was worn long this evening and shone under the lights. The dress she had chosen was black, with a low, scooped neckline. She looked sophisticated and had every intention of acting that way.

The pendant was the only piece of jewelry she wore. It was an obvious adornment, one that could hardly be ignored. She waited with interest for Eric to mention it.

Infuriatingly he talked of other things, never mentioning

the pendant, although his eyes seemed to stray more and more often to where it hung around her neck.

While Jenny picked at her meal, Eric seemed to enjoy his. There was no hint of embarrassment in his manner—no apology. But in his social circle it was probably considered the norm to sweep a woman off her feet and then abandon her summarily once his interest had waned. Eric appeared to have a short interest span.

The small talk had gone on long enough. Perhaps she had somehow still held to the ridiculous hope that he would beg her forgiveness, that he would offer an explanation for his actions—or at least make an attempt to convince her there was some rationale for the way he had behaved. But no; it was clear that she was nothing more than an evening's diversion. And that was all she had been seven months ago in Paris.

She reached up to her neck, feeling for the small clasp that would undo the pendant. Her speech had been rehearsed. She would present it, along with the necklace, and leave immediately. The unfortunate interlude with Eric Delmont would be finally completed.

Suddenly she stopped, her fingers dropping from the clasp as she stared. Something was amiss; something was wrong.

Eric didn't smoke. Yet he had just lighted a cigarette. And he had used not his right hand, but his left. Eric was not left-handed, she was sure of it.

"Is something wrong?" he asked, suddenly attentive to her changed mood.

"Wrong?" she echoed evasively, desperately needing time to think.

"You looked strange all of a sudden, like something had

upset you." There was wariness in his tone. With his left hand he flicked ashes into the small tray by his plate.

Jenny followed the action with her eyes. He was nervous. There was no need to flick ashes into a tray when you had only just lighted a cigarette.

"You said you had something to give me? You mentioned it this afternoon at the bullfight." Eric waited for her to respond.

"Yes . . . yes, I did." She watched him carefully, noticing small things about him that she had overlooked in her emotional state. She had been so concerned about how she appeared to him, that she had failed to note something amazing.

The man she sat across from, the man she had invited to dinner, and to whom she was almost ready to turn over a valuable piece of jewelry, was not the right man. He was not Eric Delmont.

"Who are you?" she asked, point-blank.

A mocking smile of amusement slowly crossed his face. "Oh, so you've finally discovered your slight oversight."

"How dare you laugh at me?" she exclaimed angrily, and started to rise.

His hand shot forward and with a firm, but unobvious jerk of her wrist, he forced her to sit again. "Don't go," he said, still smiling. "I rather enjoy your company."

Jenny seethed. "I can't say the same for yours," she remarked icily.

"Then please, think of me as Eric." The blue eyes were cold.

"I don't think that would be wise," she said. "Quite frankly, I don't find his company that compelling, either, these days. But you do have one other thing in common besides your looks."

"Really?" he replied without interest.

"Yes. You are both unbearably arrogant," she snapped and rose to leave again.

"Sit down."

Something forbidding in his voice made her comply.

"Now I've got a question for you. Where did you get that necklace?"

"It was given to me."

"By someone in Marrakesh, perhaps?"

Knowing he was watching her carefully, Jenny tried hard to hide her complete astonishment, but failed miserably. How could he possibly have known about the man who had brought back her necklace after it had been stolen? He could be with the police, but that didn't make sense. From what she knew of the countess, she had assumed that the woman had contacts in the underworld, and that she used those contacts to retrieve the necklace for her as a favor to Mr. Farrar. That meant that the only way this man, this double of Eric Delmont's, could possibly know about the necklace would be if he were somehow involved in a crime network.

"I'm waiting for your answer," he prompted impatiently.

"The necklace was stolen. It was returned to me later."

"By whom?"

"I don't know his name."

"Then think harder. I'm sure you can remember." His voice was threatening, and for the first time since that night in Marrakesh, when she'd thought she would be murdered and left in an alleyway, she was truly frightened.

"I'm telling you, I don't know his name," she insisted. "I told someone about the necklace and later a man came to my door and returned it."

"All right," the man across from her said, "we'll talk about that later. Now let's discuss Eric."

"There isn't anything to say about him. Nothing that would concern you, anyway."

"That's where you're wrong. This man does concern me. Apparently we're doubles."

"That still makes no difference to me. I want to go now."

Jenny looked at the tables nearby. People were busy talking, enjoying their meals. No one seemed to take the slightest notice of the conversation she and her dinner partner were having. She wondered what would happen if she were to make a scene.

As if tuned into her thoughts, the man spoke harshly. "You're not leaving this table until you answer my questions. And don't try to make any kind of a scene, either. I'm very well connected here, you might say. Try something, and I promise you, you'll come out on the short end."

"All right," Jenny said, having no difficulty in believing what he told her. "Eric Delmont is a man I met at a party outside Paris. We dated only one time after I first met him. There's nothing more to it than that."

"You're lying."

"It's the truth. Look, I don't know what you want of me. Whatever you're involved in is your business, okay? It doesn't concern me and I don't concern you."

"Eric concerns me."

"Why?" For the life of her, she couldn't see the logic behind his interest.

"He's someone I've wanted to meet for a long time. He's become quite a pest." The man drew deeply on his cigarette. "Where is he?"

"I don't know."

"Why do you persist in wasting my time?" he asked, and again his tone was harsh. "Give me your purse."

She handed it to him. There was nothing in it of value, so why argue? Her wallet with traveler's checks, her passport and a small address book that she had carried with her to send postcards to friends in the United States and France were the only things in it.

His hands searched through her belongings with a deft assurance born of long practice. He checked her wallet, pausing to examine her identification, and looked up at her. "Ah, Jennifer Gordon, is it? How do you do?"

She stared back at him in stony silence, outraged at the liberties he was taking.

He snapped her wallet closed and removed the small black address book. Leafing through it, he hummed softly and confidently to himself. His face clouded. He looked up at her.

"Where is it?" he said, flinging the address book down on the table.

Jenny reached for it, and put it in her lap. "If you mean Eric's address, I don't have it. I've never known where he lives," she lied. No matter what Eric had done to disappoint her personally, there was no reason to subject him to danger, and this man, she knew instinctively, was dangerous.

Even as she thought it, his mood changed. Suddenly relaxed, he snuffed out his cigarette. Smiling, he leaned against the back of his chair.

"Forgive me," he said apologetically. "I've been an abusive bore, something I find intolerable in other people. Shall we begin again? My name, dearest lady, is Jacques Montand."

Jenny was so stunned by the abrupt metamorphosis, she could find nothing to say in return.

This time he didn't push her to respond. "Any other man

in my position would have been wracking his brain to think of ways to win your favor. You're incredibly beautiful, Jennifer," he said, leaning forward and staring deeply into her eyes. He sat back again. "Instead, I'm afraid I've done nothing but make you despise me."

"You're wasting your time, Mr. Montand," she managed finally.

"Let me be the judge of that, please," he said softly, sincerity ringing from his voice.

"I have nothing to tell you," Jenny said, her voice firm.

He responded with an easy unconcern. "Perhaps not now." He waved his hand langorously. "But later, dear Jennifer, you might."

"There won't be a later."

"Again, beautiful lady . . . let me be the judge."

Jacques Montand smiled graciously, and chills traveled up and down Jenny's spine. But they weren't pleasant sensations; they carried the vibrations of fear through her body.

Chapter 9

Jenny fled from the taxi as Jacques paid the driver. She ran through her hotel lobby, halted at the bank of elevators, pushed the button to bring a car to her, and waited frantically for the door to open.

"Please. Open . . . open . . ." she whispered urgently under her breath.

The door in front of her parted. She waited for two men to disembark; she let them pass, then jumped inside the elevator, hitting the button to close the door.

The elevator bounced slightly as the doors drew together. As they finally slid shut, she glimpsed Jacques Montand. He had entered the lobby and was looking directly at her. And the look on his face wasn't pleasant.

But she was safe. The doors had shut.

Breathing a sigh of relief, she leaned into the corner of the elevator. The ride up seemed interminable. But at least she had lost him; he wouldn't be able to find her now. Or would he?

. With a shock of realization, she glanced up over the elevator door. There, in bold lights, was a record of her progress as she ascended. Jacques was downstairs no doubt watching the register over the elevator doors. He'd be able to see where the elevator stopped; he'd know where she got off.

The doors parted, letting her out on the eighth floor. She stepped into the hall, her heart pounding as she raced for her room. Even if he could track her to the right floor, he'd never know which room she was in. He couldn't wait in the hall all night. Eventually he'd have to leave, and tomorrow she could take a flight back to Paris, free forever of his unwelcome company.

She had managed to fight off his advances in the taxi. But he had been persistent, and she didn't expect him to give up his pursuit easily.

Just before her door, she turned and looked back at the elevators. The register showed that someone was on his way up. And she had no doubt as to his identity.

She opened her purse, feeling inside for her keys.

Gone! The keys weren't there! Frantic, she dumped the contents of her purse onto the floor, bent to her knees, and ran her hands through the scattered belongings.

Over her shoulder, she could see the elevator moving steadily upward. It stopped at the sixth floor. Someone else had been riding up with him.

She shook her purse wildly, desperate to locate the keys that perhaps had slipped down behind the lining. No use. They simply weren't there.

The elevator had risen again, moving to the seventh floor. She felt like a trapped animal. She couldn't stay out all night wandering the streets. He'd find her if she went back to the lobby, and the restaurants were already closed. She *had* to get into her room.

What had happened to her keys? She'd had them with her when she'd left the hotel. Her mind reeled as she desperately tried to think of what to do.

There was a slight dinging sound as the elevator hit the eighth floor. Quietly the doors slid open and a man stepped out.

Jacques Montand dangled a pair of keys in his hand, a cruel smile playing across his lips, his eyes cold and threatening.

Automatically Jenny started to back away. He walked slowly toward her, the keys jangling musically in the silent hall. Now she understood; he had taken the keys when they were in the restaurant.

He stopped in front of her and opened the door to her room.

"Shall we?" he asked pleasantly, nodding his head toward the empty room.

"Leave me alone," she pleaded. "Please."

"But, why?" He laughed, throwing the keys into the room. "Don't you want your keys? There they are; now go get them."

Jenny judged the distance she would have to go to enter her room and slam the door in his face. It was a chance she'd have to take. But if she didn't make it? No, that didn't bear thinking about. She'd just have to take the risk.

Moving rapidly, she rushed to the open door. Entering the room at a run, she slammed the door behind her. At least, that was what she tried to do, but there was no resounding noise when the door closed. Because it hadn't.

Jacques had wedged his foot between the door and the

doorjamb. She was no match for him; and now they both knew it.

He shoved the door open and entered, then closed it behind him. They were alone.

"Come here," he said, beckoning to her. His voice was soft and tinged with mockery.

"No, get out of here. Leave me alone!" she pleaded breathlessly, backing farther away from him.

"I won't hurt you. You're much, much too beautiful to hurt." He moved toward her slowly, his eyes never leaving her face.

There was nowhere for her to run. He could easily overpower her, and the room was soundproofed so a scream would do nothing more than anger him.

In a few seconds he was beside her, his hand reaching up to touch her hair. She felt his breath warm against her ear and caressing her exposed neck. Trembling with fear, she tried to move away, but he merely increased the pressure of his hold on her neck.

"Tell me where Eric Delmont is," he commanded. "Tell me."

For a moment she was stunned. He didn't want to harm her, as he had threatened earlier. He just wanted information. If she told him about the Pierre, he'd leave her alone. And if she didn't? That was something she didn't want to think about. Not yet, anyway.

"Why do you want to know?" she asked, stalling for time while she thought out her options.

"We have a debt to settle—Mr. Delmont and I."

"Why? What has Eric got to do with you?"

"Nothing. That's the problem. He's been meddling in my business, making it very difficult for me."

"What kind of business?"

"Pretty things—I deal in pretty things, things that sparkle like your eyes," he said softly, and reached around her neck for the pendant.

Of course! He was involved with the jewel thefts. That would have to be it. That was why she had seen Eric near the scene of so many crimes. He was somehow involved, too. Obviously they were in competition for the same goods.

She almost laughed out loud. She, too, had been a prey of sorts.

For the time being, though, she didn't have time to dwell on what Eric's part in the crimes might have been. She had to get rid of Jacques.

"All right," she agreed. "I'll tell you what you want to know. I'll tell you where Eric Delmont lives."

Jacques looked surprised. He dropped his hand from her neck and stepped away, but only slightly. He could still reach her in a split second, should he choose. "Good," he said and waited.

"No, not now," she hedged. "I can't give you the information now." She was stalling for time and he knew it. He took a menacing step closer, his eyes no more than narrow, glittering slits.

"I'll tell you tomorrow," she added hurriedly. "The information you want is written down in my permanent address book at home. If I call now, my mother will know something is wrong. Believe me, I know her. She worries about me when I travel, and she'd call the hotel manager immediately."

He seemed to digest her story. "All right," he agreed finally. "You've got until tomorrow morning. I'll be back here at nine. Have it ready for me."

He didn't have to add the obvious: "or you'll be sorry."

There was absolutely no doubt in her mind that she would be, too.

With vivid, horrifying clarity she remembered the story of the woman who had been robbed in her hotel suite and left to die in her room from a gunshot wound. No, she didn't doubt that she had better have the information when he returned the following morning.

She watched as he turned and walked from the room, closing the door silently behind him.

Like a thief, she thought—then realized that that was because Jacques Montand *was* a thief.

She crossed to the closed door and held her ear against the wood, listening for any sounds in the hall. All was quiet. She slid the security lock in place. She was safe. At least for the time being.

Exhausted, she sank down on the edge of her bed and mulled over the few options open to her.

She wouldn't tell Jacques where Eric lived. She couldn't. Eric had hurt her badly, had made a complete fool of her, and she certainly intended to best him at his own heartless game. But now that she knew he was in true danger, she realized feelings for him still existed.

She didn't need Anne to tell her how foolish it was to be willing to risk her own safety for a man who didn't care about her, a man who lived a life shrouded in mystery. But she had no choice. It would be impossible to live with her conscience if she put Eric's life in jeopardy.

So there was really only one alternative open to her. She would have to leave Spain immediately. If she took the earliest flight to Paris, she'd be safe, out of Jacques Montand's reach, unless—and she shuddered the chilling thought—he followed her to France.

But Paris was a big city; he'd never find her. She had to

believe that, because the thought of him tracking her down conjured up visions too frightening even to consider.

Jenny awoke at the first light of dawn. What sleep she'd had, had been troubled. Now, with her eyes open, she realized that her waking state was even worse. The face of Jacques Montand loomed before her, threateningly real.

She sat up and reached for the telephone, dialing Air France's reservation number. The representative was sorry; no seats were available on any of the early-morning flights. Tourists and businessmen had taken them all. Dismayed, she booked herself on a flight leaving for Paris at noon.

That meant she had to find something to do outside the hotel for the interim hours. It would be foolish to stay at the airport. It was the first place Jacques would think to look for her. That was only logical. With any luck, he'd probably assume she had taken an earlier flight to Paris to escape him. That, too, was logical.

She packed quickly, throwing her clothes haphazardly into her suitcase, rather than packing them neatly as was her habit.

She checked her watch. It was already seven o'clock. The arrangements with the airline had consumed too much of her precious time.

Her heart pounded wildly as she raced through her hotel room, checking to make certain she hadn't left anything. The suitcase wouldn't close. Beads of perspiration trickled down her forehead. The lock on the suitcase was stuck, half open, half closed.

At any moment a knock might sound on her door and Jacques Montand would appear. The possibility was too frightening to contemplate.

She was in a panic by now and knew she'd accomplish

nothing unless she calmed herself down. Forcing herself to sit down, she took in long, deep breaths. "Be calm, be calm," she whispered to herself over and over again. Her heartbeat slowly returned to normal and, standing, she once again tackled the problem of the suitcase.

This time the lock clicked and the suitcase sprang open. Taking infinite care, she rearranged her clothes, closed the lid, and pressing it down with one hand, quickly reached down with the other to snap the lock in place.

With a sigh of relief, she picked up the suitcase and lugged it to the door, then paused, fearful to leave her cocoon of safety. But to stay, she knew, would mean certain disaster.

There was no time to waste; each moment was precious if she were to evade Jacques Montand.

She released the safety lock on the door, turned the handle and stepped into the hall.

It was clear. A maid was at the far end, already at her routine chores of preparing rooms for new guests, but there was no sign of another human being. In particular, there was no sign of Jacques Montand.

But now she had a choice to make. If she took the elevator down, she'd risk coming face-to-face with Jacques, who might even now be on his way up in one of the elevators. And that one would be the first to stop at her floor. The stairway at the end of the hall would be safer for her purposes, but much slower, and the bag she carried was heavy.

There wasn't any choice, not really. She'd have to take the stairs.

There was only one man helping customers at the cashier's desk when Jenny finally arrived in the lobby. A small line had formed already. She was fourth, behind a Swedish man arguing vigorously with his wife. Five minutes later, the man at the front of the line being helped by the lone employee walked away. The other customers moved ahead, shuffling their suitcases forward with their feet.

Long, nerve-racking minutes went by before Jenny had her turn. During that time, she felt she had died a hundred times. With each swing of the entrance door in the lobby, she trembled and held her breath, expecting to see the man she feared. Each time, she let out a sigh of relief as someone she'd never seen before passed through the door. It was akin to playing Russian roulette; with each blank she felt safe, but as each one passed, the odds narrowed and the danger multiplied.

At last it was her turn at the cashier's desk. She paid quickly. A porter approached her to offer assistance with her bag. She declined, almost rudely, so intent was she on fleeing from the hotel as fast as possible.

A line of taxis waiting for new fares were parked fifty yards from the hotel's entrance. She hailed one.

The man moved slowly to his car, turning back once or twice to confer with the other drivers, who were still lounging in small groups as they gossiped and smoked, waiting for their passengers.

Farther down the street a black car turned the corner. Two men sat in the front seat, the driver and a passenger, staring out the window, pointing ahead to the hotel. Even from that distance, Jenny did not need to be told who he was. Jacques Montand had come for her.

The taxi driver opened the front door to his cab.

Move, move, Jenny urged him mentally. She picked up her suitcase and began to run toward him.

The black car was coming faster now. Jacques was looking straight ahead, directly at her, and she saw his lips curl into an angry snarl.

The cab driver revved up his engine. It gave a feeble growl, turning over like a sleep-laden man unhappily disturbed. Finally, the taxi pulled away from the curb.

Beyond it, the black car was racing closer, ever closer. There was a sudden screech of tires as it came to a stop just behind the cab pulling out from the side of the road.

Jenny stepped from the sidewalk and grasped the back-door handle of the cab.

"Stop!"

It was a man's voice, and she turned to see Jacques Montand burst from the front seat of the black car. Without wasting another second, she wrenched open the taxi's door and flung the heavy suitcase across the seat, piling in after it. Slamming the door behind her, she smashed her fist down hard on the lock. Just in time.

Jacques tore at the door handle. Quickly she leaned over the front seat and secured its lock, as well, then screamed at the driver to go, and go fast.

The man shot her a puzzled look, as if deliberating on whether he wanted to become involved in her obvious predicament.

"Go! Please!"

Her desperate insistence turned the tide of indecision. The cab driver gave her a broad smile, turned forward, and with a lurch and a screech of rubber on pavement, sped off.

Jacques Montand was left behind in the street, his fist raised in an upright, warning gesture. Jenny saw him race to the black car just as the taxi hurtled around a corner, cutting off her view.

There was no time to congratulate herself on having escaped. She had to find a place to hide. Taxis were fine for going to and from airports, but she didn't have enough cash on her to drive through the city until noon.

Without slowing, the cab driver aimed his car through the streets at a hair-raising clip. Driving well was obviously a point of honor among his compatriots, and "well" meant stopping on dimes, executing turns on two wheels, and cutting in and out of traffic with only inches to spare between cars.

Fifteen minutes later she instructed him to let her out. She paid him, tipping him well, and thanked him profusely for his help. Were it not for his driving prowess, she'd be in the hands of Jacques Montand at that very moment. But there was no chance that she had been followed.

Smells of freshly baked bread emanated from a small café near the Prado, Madrid's famous art museum. She'd have some coffee and wait for the museum to open.

No one would think of looking for her there, she was sure. Jacques had probably headed for the airport already, thinking she'd be leaving to catch a plane. Possibly he'd wait for the first two flights to depart and then, with any luck, would become discouraged when she didn't appear. By the time she did arrive at the airport for her noon flight, he'd be safe. He would have given up and gone elsewhere to find her.

Even the smell of the warm bread failed to stimulate her appetite. Her stomach felt balled into a tight, hard knot. All her senses were alive to her surroundings; each face at a nearby table was a possible enemy, every voice was that of a pursuer. Fear had made her wary of the most ordinary gesture.

She consoled herself with the knowledge that in a few hours she'd be back in Paris, safe and sound. Then all of this could be forgotten. Perhaps she would be wise to follow Anne's advice. She would forget Eric Delmont, wash her hands of him entirely. But although this was probably the safest decision, she knew it would not satisfy her curiosity, nor the longing still in her heart to see Eric once more under normal circumstances.

From her place at the table Jenny could see out onto the street through the café's plate-glass windows. She looked on in sudden interest as police cars assembled outside the museum. Something was obviously going on. Curious onlookers had assembled on the outskirts of the main sphere of activity.

A woman entered the café, shaking her head back and forth, and took a table next to Jenny's.

"It is terrible," she said to the young waiter who approached and suggested the rolls, along with an order of eggs, for breakfast. "A Goya. The beasts took it."

The waiter looked outside at the crowded sidewalk in front of the Prado.

"Or perhaps, " added the woman somewhat vaguely, "it could have been a Velasquez." She wasn't sure of her painters, she mentioned confidentially.

The waiter returned to the kitchen. A moment later another man, this one older, and whom Jenny assumed to be the owner, approached the woman's table and spoke to her in rapid Spanish, making it difficult for Jenny to follow the conversation. She heard him ask, "How?"

"They stayed in there all night, that's how," the woman said indignantly. "Yes, they were locked up with all the paintings, free to choose whichever one they wanted," she clucked. "This morning they took the Goya, or whatever it was, with them. They left the museum when the guard changed from night to morning."

The man's reaction was one of outraged disbelief. "Im

possible!" he bellowed, looking past his customers into the street beyond.

"It is not! That is what happened!" the woman countered vigorously, as if her honor had been impugned.

"But the guards are there all night. I, myself, serve them their dinners."

"Well," replied the woman huffily, "that may be. But the Goya is still missing!"

The man shook his head mournfully.

"Next time," she went on, "perhaps you should not stuff the night watch, making them so sleepy they spend their time snoring on the job instead of watching. All of Spain would thank you for that!"

"Never mind," said the man. "The thieves will be caught. No one could escape with such a treasure and go undetected for long."

He turned and walked back to his kitchen, shaking his head in dismay and muttering under his breath.

Thieves.

Not thief, singular; thieves, plural. Jenny's mind was already hard at work, fitting pieces of the puzzle together.

Jacques Montand was in town and once more a theft had occurred. That meant that very possibly another person was in town—Eric Delmont. Hadn't Jacques complained about Eric meddling in his business? And Jacques Montand had more or less admitted he was in the business of stealing.

Had Eric beaten Jacques to the punch, so to speak? It was obvious that Jacques couldn't have committed this crime, because he had been with her the previous evening, and the woman had said the thieves had been locked in the museum when it closed.

That left Eric.

Except . . . the term used was thieves. Whoever had

committed the daring theft hadn't worked alone. Jacques could have accomplices. He didn't actually have to involve himself physically.

She remembered the other man in the car with Jacques that morning. Perhaps there were others who worked for him and were involved in the crime. Jacques had made himself very visible the previous night. He had chosen an expensive restaurant, one in which he was personally known. He'd insisted she stay, and part of that reason might have been that he'd wanted to use her as part of his alibi.

No, Jacques Montand could not be entirely absolved of the theft of the Goya. But, then, neither could Eric.

Jenny thought back on her visit to Eric's sumptuous apartment at the Pierre Hotel. The walls had been covered in priceless paintings, some by master artists. Was he a mad collector, hoarding treasures for himself? That was a fanciful notion, but hardly realistic. Most men willing to risk their freedom and their lives in this manner were in it for one thing, and one thing only: money.

It was clear that both Jacques and Eric appreciated the finer things in life. Yet Jacques had appeared sinister, whereas Eric had been open and warm.

She was being foolish again: Eric had been this; Eric had been that. The question was, what was Eric really?

Jenny glanced at her watch. It was ten-thirty. She had entered the museum as soon as it had opened. Guards and police were everywhere. Several of the rooms were closed, and only those that had been carefully examined were opened to visitors.

Now it was time to go. She'd have to take a cab back to the airport, allow time for flight arrangements to be made, and check her luggage. Over the past few hours she had begun to feel safe again. All she had to do now was to get on that plane and she'd be free of Jacques Montand.

The airport was jammed. Tourists were everywhere, and any space they didn't occupy was filled by bustling businessmen and airport employees. Her suitcase seemed unbearably heavy. This time she allowed a porter to assist her.

Arrangements for her flight went smoothly and she found herself with half an hour to spare before boarding would begin.

She entered the duty-free store to purchase gifts for Allan and Michael, and found a lovely lace shawl for her mother. As she left she looked up, suddenly aware of a man standing against a pole in the terminal. A newspaper covered his face, but she was certain that a moment before he had been staring directly at her.

She walked quickly toward the airport restaurant. From the corner of her eye, she saw the man lower the newspaper to his side and walk in the same direction she had taken. She didn't recognize him, but was convinced he was following her.

Entering the restaurant, she found a line of people all waiting to be seated by the hostess.

The man was still behind her.

Without waiting, she cut in front of the other customers and walked into the main body of the room. She stood on tiptoe and turned her head in various directions, as if looking for a friend.

Toward the back of the room, a woman sat by herself at a small table. Jenny moved toward her and stopped at the table. "May I sit down, please?" she asked.

The woman looked, obviously slightly annoyed at the intrusion.

"Please? I have to catch a plane in a few minutes, and—"(she looked toward the line of people, seeing that the man with the newspaper stood slightly beyond them at the edge of the restaurant "—I really need to eat something. I don't feel well," she lied.

"Very well," the woman said grudgingly, still annoyed.

Jenny sat. A waiter appeared shortly afterward and she ordered orange juice, realizing too late that the woman probably expected her to order something more substantial after what she'd said about not feeling well.

Mentally she gave a small shrug and looked up. The line was shorter now. The man holding the newspaper was to be seated next.

The woman opposite her looked at her curiously, and for the first time Jenny realized that her forehead was covered with beads of perspiration. No doubt the woman now believed her story about being sick.

Jenny saw the hostess smile cordially to the man who had been following her, his newspaper still wadded like a club and held at his side. He followed the hostess across the room, his eyes scanning every table.

As he neared hers, Jenny slammed a fist full of change onto the table to cover her drink and bolted for the door leading from the restaurant back into the terminal.

She saw the man whirl around, but had no time to watch what he did next. She had to get out, and as far away from him as possible.

The terminal was busy, thronged with people greeting friends and relatives; others checked their watches and paced the room, waiting for planes either to arrive or depart.

A female voice came onto the loudspeaker. Her flight was boarding at last.

She searched for the gate number she was to report at. The man appeared on the periphery of her vision. He had followed her from the restaurant and he, too, was looking around. Only he was looking for her.

Frantically Jenny rushed ahead. There was no time to waste; she had to get on board the plane to Paris. Unless he had purchased a ticket, which was unlikely, she'd then be safe.

She went through the security system, passing easily and rapidly through the metal detector and then through a door leading to the plane that would take her to safety.

Just before she passed through the door leading to the plane, she turned around. She'd been right; the man didn't have a ticket. He was beyond the security checkpoint, glaring at her, and this time, she did recognize him. It was the man who had been with Jacques Montand that morning.

Chapter 10

Jenny had arrived home, emotionally and physically exhausted. The Paris newspapers were filled with reports of the stolen painting; a Goya, as it turned out.

She didn't dare tell her stepmother about the incident in Madrid. There was no need for them both to worry. As it was, her mother looked tired and drawn, barely having recovered from a summer cold that had hung on for over a month.

Anne, she learned, was engaged to Quentin. Monica was mopey as always. Allan and Michael had entered upon an ambitious program of putting together their own homemade telescope, certain of spotting unidentified flying objects in the sky the moment it was assembled.

On the surface everything appeared normal. But Jenny could feel an undercurrent of tension building up.

She was frightened. She had returned from Madrid satisfied that she had escaped Jacques Montand. Finding her in Paris would be like looking for the proverbial needle in the haystack. Yet, several things had occurred during the past week to cause her alarm.

Allan had been playing in the park near their home when a strange man had approached him. He'd began a conversation by talking of sports, but it hadn't been long before the conversation had turned to other things—more personal things, relating to Allan's family. Did his mother work? How many brother and sisters did he have at home? "Things like that," Allan had told her.

By the time the young lad had realized he was being pumped for information, too much personal data had been disclosed.

"Why did he want to know all that stuff, anyway?" he asked his stepsister.

"Maybe he's just curious about how other people live," Jenny answered reassuringly.

But she was far from reassured herself. Of course, it could have been coincidence. A lonely man meets a young boy in the park and tries to recapture his own childhood by making friends. On the other hand, someone could be trying to find out information about her.

Two days later her worst suspicions were confirmed. Someone broke into the office. Monica was furious when Jenny entered the travel agency at nine o'clock that morning. Both their desks had been ransacked, papers had been emptied from drawers, files had been ravaged. But only a small amount of money had been taken from the petty-cash box, and none of the expensive business machines had been stolen.

"What on earth do you think they could have wanted from a travel agency?" Monica asked, putting her telephone card file back in alphabetical order.

Jenny shook her head. "I don't know." But she did. They wanted information. About her.

Then, for a week, life continued without any additional disruptions. One Tuesday morning Mr. Farrar called Jenny into his office.

"I've got a problem," he began. "Sit down."

Jenny sat in the chair facing his desk.

"I've got thirty boys who are planning on spending a week in the French Alps and no one to take them up there."

It wasn't hard to see where the conversation was headed. Jenny groaned inwardly and squirmed uncomfortably in her seat. She loved children . . . but thirty boys?

"You know what I'm getting at, don't you?" he asked, leaning back in his chair and fiddling with a paper clip from off his desk.

"Yes, and it sounds dreadful."

"It's absolutely necessary." It was, and she knew it. This was the first of a series of get-away vacations for younger travelers that he had organized. Money had been spent on printing brochures and on mailings. She couldn't let him down. But, oh, it wasn't going to be easy.

"All right," she agreed, reluctant to the point of sheer, absolute dread.

"Fine! I knew I could count on you." He smiled happily.

"That is, all right, on one condition."

Mr. Farrar's smile faded slightly. "Yes?" he queried hesitantly.

"I'd like to take advantage of one of those free trips the hotels offer to Portugal."

"But, why? You've been to Portugal twice this year already."

"It's not for me. It's for my mother. She's exhausted, and I'd like to give her a surprise vacation."

It was arranged.

Her mother left for Portugal the following Tuesday morning. Jenny was to depart on Friday, leaving Anne in charge of Allan and Michael. Plans were made, bags packed—and disaster struck.

Anne couldn't come. A family crisis had reared its ugly, inconvenient head and Anne was needed at home to lend moral support to her mother. She was desperately sorry, but there wasn't anything she could do. Jenny understood, but it made things difficult, to say the least.

Monica was the only hope she had, and surprisingly her co-worker agreed to come over for the weekend and play guardian at Jenny's house.

"Thanks," said Jenny, not quite succeeding in keeping the astonishment out of her voice.

"It's no big deal. I didn't have anything to do, anyway." Monica shrugged, looking slightly embarrassed by her own uncharacteristic generosity.

"Oh, but it is," Jenny countered. "And I really appreciate the favor. Just remember, it won't be forever! I'll be back Sunday night to rescue you from the two mad astronomers."

THE TRIP ON THE BUS had been nerve-racking in the extreme. Monica didn't know what a good deal she had. Jenny deposited her thirty wriggling, shouting, singing, pinching, punching charges to the care of four stalwart-looking camp counselors and rushed back to Paris. And to peace and quiet.

It was dark when she arrived home, but the lights inside looked cheery as she approached the house.

"I'm back," she called, throwing the light sweater she had worn home over the back of a chair. She placed her overnight case on the floor and looked around for signs of life.

Monica came through the kitchen door. Allan followed close behind her.

"Hi," greeted Jenny "And where's the third musketeer?"

"Michael went with Eric Delmont." Allan grinned broadly, pleased to have made the announcement.

"Shh . . . let me tell her." Monica ruffled the top of his head, her eyes on Jenny, whose face had turned ashen.

She couldn't speak. After so long, after so many months of wishing and hoping and finally giving up, Eric had reappeared in her life. And now that it had happened, she didn't know how to respond. She sat down on the couch, staring straight ahead, but seeing nothing as she tried to put her thoughts in order.

Monica walked over and stood in front of her, looking down with a curious expression on her face, half pleased, half worried.

"You see," she began, "the boys were outside playing in the frontyard. They were testing the telescope—which works, incidentally." She paused and shook her head in wonder. "Anyway, I went ouside, and there was a man there."

"Eric?"

"Yes. I didn't know who he was at first, of course. I'm afraid I thought the worst, seeing a stranger in the yard. But when we started speaking, he told me his name—Eric Delmont. I knew it would be all right if I let Michael go with him."

"Where? Where did he take Michael?"

"Out for some supplies. The stores were still open and he said he'd help Michael shop for some things they needed for the telescope."

"I wanted to go, too," Allan said. "He wouldn't let me, though."

Jenny turned her head and looked at him curiously. "But why?"

Something was very wrong. Eric had no way of knowing where she lived. And why wouldn't he take Allan with him?

"He said it would be faster if just two people went. I didn't think it made much sense, but I didn't argue about it because Michael really wanted to get the extra lens and some screws we needed."

"You're upset," said Monica, a puzzled frown creasing her forehead. "I thought you'd be happy. I thought for once I'd done something right."

Jenny stood and paced back and forth by the window, looking out, afraid to voice the obvious. Eric Delmont hadn't picked up Michael. Another man had. Jacques Montand.

She thought back to the evening at the El Cordoba. He had taken her purse and had obviously memorized not only her home address, but her work address, as well. What a fool she had been to think she had escaped from him. It would have been more convenient for him if he'd apprehended her in Spain, to be sure, but not entirely necessary.

"Monica, did Eric ever call me at the office?" she asked suddenly, whirling to face the other woman.

Monica's face paled.

"The truth, Monica!" insisted Jenny vehemently. "This is important. You aren't just getting back at me anymore, you'd be hurting a child."

The other woman's face crumbled and she slumped into the couch, cupping her face in her hands. "I'm so ashamed. Yes," she whispered, "he did call." She raised her face and looked directly into Jenny's eyes.

"Eric really did call?"

"He called right after you met him."

"Why on earth didn't you tell me before this?" Jenny's anger was intense, but the thought that she had not been wrong about Eric caring for her provided some solace at least, leaving her with a feeling of sad irony.

Great tears hung, waiting to fall from the rims of Monica's eyes. "I know, I know," she said miserably. "It was rotten of me. I was so unhappy. I hated myself for being such a failure. And there you were. Beautiful, talented, loved. You were everything I wanted to be and I hated you for it." She rose, the tears flowing freely, her face anguished.

Jenny turned away. She felt sorry for Monica, but right now she could neither understand nor forgive the misery she had caused her. Monica walked closer, forcing Jenny to look at her.

"I wanted to tell you for the longest while. Really. But I couldn't. I knew how furious you'd be. And you'd have had every right."

"What did you say when he called?" Jenny had to force herself to speak calmly.

"I told him you didn't work at our travel agency. I told him—oh, God, Jenny—I told him I had never heard of you."

Jenny grabbed hold of the drapery, squeezing the fabric tightly within her fist. Eric must have thought she had lied to him. He must have thought that she didn't want to see him again and had given him a phony telephone number. All this time he must have been thinking she had scorned him.

Outside the sky was black. Jenny watched dark clouds, tall and ominous, gathering against the lighter shade of night, cutting off the stars and moon, just as Monica had cut off Eric from being a part of her life.

"How many times did he call me?" she asked, finally turning to look at Monica.

"Twice—no, three times. Each time I said I'd never heard of you."

"Until finally he stopped calling," murmured Jenny sadly.

Monica shook her head. "But, Jenny, it's all right now. Eric will be back any minute with Michael," she said with forced brightness, glancing at the darkened sky beyond the window. "You'll see each other again. Blame it all on me. It's my fault. Listen, I'll tell him the truth. I'll tell him, Jenny, I promise."

"Monica! Stop it!"

The other woman flinched. "That's all right, yell. I deserve it."

"Don't you see, Monica?" said Jenny urgently. "Don't you understand that Eric Delmont isn't the man who took Michael away from the house tonight? He couldn't have. Because Eric Delmont doesn't know where I live. All he knows is my name and where I work, and you didn't tell him anything else about me."

"Then, who . . . " began Monica.

"Another man," Jenny interrupted swiftly. She glanced at Allan and saw at once that he seemed to be understanding the severity of the situation more clearly than Monica. "Allan, I want to talk to Monica privately. We have a lot of things to clear up between us."

She waited for her brother to leave, then continued.

"The man who took Michael is a criminal. He's Eric's double, and he's desperate to find him. I can't tell you the whole story now, but believe me, this man will stop at nothing to get his way."

"But why would this man want Michael?" asked Monica, obviously completely mystified.

"He doesn't. He wants me. I have information that he needs. Only I'm not going to give it to him."

"Maybe you should."

Yes, Jenny thought, maybe I should. As it stood now, she was torn between two people she loved, the guardian of both their lives.

"What can we do now?" Monica looked as helpless as Jenny felt.

"I don't know." she said, sitting again and studying the backs of her hands as she thought. "He won't harm Michael, or he wouldn't have anything to bargain with. At least he won't harm him yet."

"I'm calling the police!" Monica rushed to get her purse.

"No!" exclaimed Jenny, springing to her feet. "We have to wait. If we do anything, it may only make matters worse for Michael."

She walked wearily up the stairs to her room and lay on her bed, staring at the ceiling. Below her, she heard Monica moving through the house, pushing furniture as she cleaned, needing something to occupy her as they waited for Jacques Montand to carry out his plan.

At close to midnight she appeared at Jenny's bedroom door. The light from the hallway was behind her, but even through the shadow that covered her face, Jenny could see fear.

She sat up, suddenly alert. "What is it?" she asked quickly.

"Someone left this. There was a knock on the door. An envelope was left outside." Monica handed the envelope to Jenny. "I didn't see anyone; whoever delivered it had already gone."

Jenny switched on the light by her nightstand and looked down at the plain brown envelope. It was thin, but then she hadn't expected Jacques to send a long, explanatory letter. There wasn't a bargain to be made in this case. She had to do what he wanted.

The contents were neatly typed, professional, impersonal and to the point.

> The boy is well. No harm will come to him. You must do as I say. Go to work tomorrow. Wait to be contacted. Do not call police, or I cannot be responsible for your brother's safety.

No signature. But it was hardly necessary.

AT NINE O'CLOCK the following morning Jenny arrived for work.

It was important to follow her normal routine. Every movement she made was probably being observed by someone, somewhere.

She couldn't risk the chance that something she did would be misconstrued as a threat to Jacques Montand. She knew now that he didn't work alone; and she knew that he was desperate enough to go to the drastic length of kidnapping a child. He was dangerous, and Michael was in his hands.

Monica had called in sick, insisting on remaining at Jenny's home with Allan. Mr. Farrar grumbled and called in a worker from a temporary agency.

Jenny couldn't keep her eyes off the clock. By eleven her nerves were alive to the slightest sound. Whenever the telephone rang, she grabbed each call with lightning speed. Still no word from Jacques Montand.

Lunchtime arrived. She didn't want to leave the office, but she knew that if she didn't, it might arouse suspicion.

Reluctantly she cleared her desk and was preparing to leave when the telephone rang. The blond woman from the agency answered, looked back at Jenny questioningly, then said to the caller, "I think she just left for lunch."

"No, I'll take it," Jenny said, grabbing the receiver. She must have appeared distraught and was immediately sorry, for the woman backed away as if alarmed by her aberrant behavior. And she couldn't afford to have anyone question her actions.

A man's voice came on the telephone. "Are you there?" it queried. It wasn't the voice she expected; it wasn't Jacques Montand.

"This is Jenny Gordon," she confirmed.

"Meet me at the duck pond in the park near your office," the man said. "It will take you seven minutes to walk there."

"How will I know—" She was about to ask how she could recognize him, when the caller hung up. Obviously there wasn't any need for her to recognize him, he knew her.

The park was a haven of greenery. Benches dotted the landscape and old people sat enjoying the warm breeze that floated the smell of blooming flowers to every visitor.

Jenny walked rapidly to the duck pond, a large man-made pool of water with a small man-made island in its center. Ducks and swans sailed lazily over the smooth surface, as if aware they were the source of entertainment for the elderly spectators onshore.

She stopped several feet to one side of the pond and surveyed the area for the man she was to meet. There was a nurse with two small children, several mothers with rowdy youngsters in tow, but no likely candidate for her contact.

On the other side of the pond, a man came out of a heavily wooded path and into a clearing. He carried a bag with French bread sticking out from its top. He was not young, but neither was he old. Sturdy and muscular, he walked purposefully toward Jenny with a springy gait, passing the benches of nodding and laughing elderly persons, sidestepping the aggressive ducks pecking at his legs for handouts.

"Let's go over here," he said, having at last arrived at her side.

She followed him to a vacant bench.

For a moment he didn't speak, but busied himself with the task of breaking off a hunk of French bread and handing it to her, cutting another piece for himself, and examining a chunk of cheese wrapped in red cellophane.

"No, thank you," Jenny demurred, pushing away the proferred cheese and bread.

"Take it, take it," the man said easily, his eyes scanning the surrounding area.

Reluctantly Jenny accepted his offer, afraid that noncompliance with even his smallest request might worsen an already desperate situation. There was Michael to consider.

The man took a bite of bread and chewed noisily. "So, you've been a good girl, Miss Gordon. My congratulations."

Jenny didn't respond. As far as she was concerned this was going to be his show. All she needed was to know what she had to do to secure her young brother's release.

"You know, I don't really like this new twist, taking a kid and all, so I hope you make things easy for us."

"What am I supposed to do?" she asked in a soft voice.

"Yeah, do. Well," he said, crinkling his eyes at the sun, "what you have to do is very simple."

"Tell me."

"You have to come with me. We'll take a little ride together and then you'll see an old friend."

"Jacques Montand."

"He's very anxious to talk to you." The man looked at her. "You caused him a bit of trouble in Madrid, you know, running out like that. Things could have been so much simpler for you. And the boy," he added meaningfully.

"All right. You've made your point." Jenny was ready to get on with it; he annoyed her. "I fully realize the situation I'm in. I know I have to do what you say, or my brother . . . my brother . . . ." Her voice choked on the words.

"Good." The man rose, taking the bag of bread and putting the cheese inside. He turned over the edges of the bag and wound it tightly to the end. "Then I don't have to give you the whole speech. Just remember this: no police, no trouble for us. That means no trouble for you."

Jenny followed him away from the bench. "What about my job?" she asked. "They'll be worried if I don't return."

"Didn't you know?" he laughed. "You've got the flu." He kicked at a stone lying in his path.

"I'm afraid they might think something was wrong and—"

"Don't worry; it's been handled, I tell you." The man leaned closer to her, parodying conspiracy. "We called in your regrets."

"But my voice?"

"The blond woman took the message. She'll say that you

called in to say you were sick. We had a lady friend of ours do the honors. Very simple."

"Oh." There seemed nothing more to say.

Jenny walked beside the man, realizing for the first time that by going with him she was not just rescuing Michael, she was putting her own life in danger. She heard the laughter of young children playing a game of tag beyond a heavy barrier of shrubbery. Overhead the sky was a brilliant blue. The air was filled with life, happiness, the promise of endless carefree days. At least for some people.

At the edge of the park, the man stopped abruptly and looked around. The street was twenty feet ahead and filled with the frantic traffic of workers intent on cramming a day's errands into a sixty-minute lunch break.

"Let's go," he said, pointing to the street. He moved ahead, evidently secure in the knowledge that she would follow.

Jenny walked hurriedly to keep pace. *This is ridiculous*, she thought, beginning to feel angry. She was an untethered hostage, agreeably following her captor to meet her fate. But what else could she do?

As they neared the street, a gray Citroën slowed and stopped at the curb, its motor idling. There was an instant blaring of horns, as drivers of other vehicles were forced to maneuver around the stationary vehicle. The man behind the Citroën's wheel remained completely unperturbed.

Jenny recognized him from Madrid, for it was the man who had driven Jacques in the black car. There was no sign of recognition on his face as he stared at her through the window.

The man she had followed from the park opened the back door of the car. "In there," he commanded, pointing to the seat behind the driver.

The free-spirited sound of the children playing mixed

with the drone of traffic. Jenny hesitated before following
the him then did as she was told. Again, there was no alternative.

The Citroën pulled away from the curb, moving through
the traffic at a speed faster than normal, yet not fast
enough to draw attention. No one had spoken.

The man beside her opened the bag of bread and cheese,
again breaking off a piece for himself, and stared out the
window as they continued through the city.

They had reached the suburbs when the driver looked
over his shoulder to his compatriot in the back seat.

"Yeah, yeah," the man next to Jenny grunted. "I know."

Jenny followed the direction of his hands as they moved
underneath the seat in front of him. Still chewing on a
piece of bread, he pulled out a small brown sack, opened it
and dumped its contents into his lap.

"Turn around," he said.

She obeyed. Using a soft rope, he tied her hands behind
her—quickly, expertly. The knot was drawn tight, and she
found that if she strained, more pressure was exerted, making the effort to free herself a futile and painful exercise.

He twisted a small plaid scarf between both his hands,
twirling it rapidly in the air to form a narrow roll, then
leaned toward her and tied the blindfold over her eyes.

There was nothing she could do; no defense was at her
disposal. Not as long as they had Michael. She was completely and utterly helpless.

She started suddenly as she felt the man's hands on her
back. He pitched her forward on the seat, adjusting her
position so that her head rested against the car's
upholstery.

From the feel of the automobile's motion, she guessed
they had taken an expressway and were now driving rapid-

ly in a fairly constant direction. After what seemed like an eternity, the car at last began to slow, cruised at a slower speed for a while, then turned and bounced its way over a rough road. It was at least another fifteen minutes before they came to a complete standstill.

With the motor turned off, she could hear the man in the front seat moving around. The door opened, and he got out of the car. She heard his feet on gravel, fading away, then the uneven thump and shuffle of someone climbing a series of steps. In the background she could hear sounds of country life. Cows lowed, presumably in a field nearby; birds rushed overhead, calling to each other.

A few moments later a door slammed and she heard more footsteps, this time approaching the car. A draft hit her as the door beside her was wrenched open and someone returned her to an upright posture. A knife sliced through the rope at her wrists and the blindfold was removed.

She was not surprised to see Jacques Montand. With one hand resting against the top of the Citroën, he leaned comfortably into the car, for all the world like a polite host welcoming his visitor after an arduous journey.

"Ah, Jennifer Gordon. How nice that you could join us."

Jenny returned his comment with a frozen silence, knowing she was better off if she kept the anger she felt to herself.

"Come," he said, offering his hand, "we have much to discuss between us."

Refusing his assistance, she pushed herself from the car, gritting her teeth against the pain as blood rushed back into those parts of her body cut off from circulation during her recent bondage.

The journey's destination turned out to be a dilapidated

farmhouse, stripped of its paint, surrounded by green pastures and isolated from any other structure for as far as the eye could see. A driveway, once apparently well-maintained and covered in white pea gravel, had partially eroded to its natural earthen state, and deep ruts appeared as past evidence of automobiles mired in mud during rains.

She was led into a sunny yellow room off a small hallway. Drapes of white organza were now torn and yellowed and hung forlornly at the sides of tall, narrow windows that overlooked the pastures beyond. What was left of the sparsely furnished room was run-down and anti-quated. Two armchairs, their stuffing visible through rips and tears, faced a sofa that tilted precariously on its three remaining legs. Likewise a player piano, with wood weathered from the sun beating against it through the un-protected windows, and missing ivory keys at random in-tervals, was pushed against a far wall.

Jacques moved about the room, stopping at each win-dow to check the outside view. "Sit down," he said, not looking directly at her.

"Thank you; I'll stand," she replied coldly.

"Suit yourself." He turned. Electric blue eyes sparked anger from across the room. "Just remember, I don't have much time," he warned. "I would advise you not to be too stubborn this time. It wouldn't be healthy."

Jenny felt her legs grow weak beneath her. Moving closer to one of the chairs, she held its back for support.

"You did a very stupid thing in Madrid, running from me like that. Now you have only yourself to blame for what happens."

"My brother? Where is he?"

"Your brother, Michael, is not here," he replied in a flat voice. "But so far he is well."

"What do you want from me?" she asked weakly, knowing the answer, but stalling for time.

"You know very well what I want," he snarled and Jenny flinched at the undisguised violence in his voice. "Don't waste my time. The stupid, naive female trick isn't going to work. I have better things to do with my time than to hole myself up in this godforsaken hovel." He looked about him with disdain.

"I can't tell you anything about Eric. That's why I left Madrid. I knew you wouldn't believe me, just as you don't believe me now."

In some ways she spoke the truth; she couldn't tell Jacques anything about Eric, because to do so meant jeopardizing the life of the man she loved. And although she might never be a part of his life, the thought that somewhere, sometime, they might meet again and resume the relationship she still prayed was real, was enough to keep her from betraying him.

But then, there was Michael to consider.

It was an insoluble, intolerable situation but one that would have to be faced sooner or later, for as Jacques had so forcefully pointed out, he didn't want to waste his time.

Suddenly, curiously, Jacques smiled, bringing his hands together at the base of his chin, a gesture of prayerful contemplation. His head was bowed in deliberation. Then, raising his eyes once again, he studied Jenny's face.

"Ah! Of course," he remarked softly. "You can't tell me about Eric, because you're afraid of implicating yourself. You're part of his operation, aren't you? The job as a travel agent is only a front for, shall we say more lucrative ventures?"

Jenny felt suddenly faint as she realized he was calling Eric a thief. The question that had haunted her for the many months she had met him was finally answered. There was no question anymore. The man she loved was definitely a criminal, just like the man standing before her and holding her brother hostage.

"There's no need for you to worry, pretty Jenny," he said, walking slowly toward her, his hand outstretched. "Come, sit. We can work out our own financial arrangement. Not only that," he went on excitedly, "but by eliminating 'friend' Delmont, there will be much more for us all the way around."

Meekly Jenny allowed him to take hold of her hand and lead her to the chair. She sat and looked up at him, wondering what her next move should be. Clearly this new proposition, though ludicrous and bizarre beyond belief, might give her a new angle from which to bargain. But it was a dangerous game to try to deceive a master of deceit.

"You're a beautiful woman. Beautiful," crooned Jacques, stroking her hair as he stood beside her. "Whatever you want, we could obtain together. All the money, all the jewels, all the art! Yes, we could have it all," he continued excitedly, evidently living the fantasy in his mind. "First we must eliminate that colossal pest, Delmont. The man is everywhere at once, and unfortunately, of late, he has been one step ahead of me."

Jenny didn't hesitate. "All right," she said, the two words sounding ominous in her ears.

"Yes?" Jacques seemed surprised. "Yes," he repeated. "Then we must begin to make plans at once."

"First you must let my brother go," she told him firmly. "Then you'll have to let me go back to Paris to collect the information that will help you. Us," she corrected, and gave him what she hoped was a becoming smile.

"No," he countered swiftly. "First you tell me where I can find Eric Delmont."

"But, I can't," she protested, praying her dismay wasn't obvious. "That is, he's moved and I have no way of locating him." That at least was the truth. "Look, I have much more valuable information. Schedules, floor plans of some of the wealthiest estates in France—England, too," she elaborated. "Museums and fine stores . . . ."

She spoke excitedly, afraid that if she hesitated for a moment to consider the folly of what she was doing, she would break down and expose her ruse, making things even worse for herself—and Michael.

"All I have to do is go back to Paris, don't you see?" she continued in a pleading tone. "There's a hiding place where we store our plans."

"Fine. Then you and I can collect the plans together."

"No!"

A wave of suspicion crossed his face. Jenny fought to control the panic that was rising within her.

"The information is in a bank vault. It would be impossible for you to accompany me—or to retrieve the information alone," she added, fearful that he would lock her away while he went to Paris.

Jacques walked away from her, pausing by a window to look outside. A tense silence hung in the room like a guillotine poised above her head, ready to slice. Without turning, he spoke in a low, measured voice.

"Tomorrow you and I will travel to Paris. We will get the papers together."

"But—"

"There are no buts," he interjected harshly. "There is only what I say. And I am telling you what we will do tomorrow. You and I . . . together."

Jenny's heart sank dismayed. Now she had really done it. His murderous rage when he discovered she had led him on a wild-goose chase, wasting his valuable time, as he'd put it, was too frightening to contemplate. And Michael! What would become of Michael?

"My brother, Michael . . . could you let him go? Now? Please," she begged.

He shook his head. "Do you find me a fool?"

"He's just a little boy. It's not fair," she pleaded, knowing her heart would break if anything happened to her brother. He was totally innocent, and it was all her fault he was now in danger. If she hadn't been so confoundedly stubborn, and had accepted the good advice of her friend, Anne, to forget Eric Delmont and find someone else, then none of this would have happened. But no. She had held onto her romantic notions of her knight in shining armor, even when all the clues pointed to the fact that he was nothing more than a vagabond in expensive clothes paid for with stolen currency.

HER WATCH READ FIVE O'CLOCK. Soon it would be dark. Jenny looked from the small window in the room at the end of the hall where she had been placed. The door had been locked from the outside, and there was no handle on the inside.

She had played right into Jacques's hands. What a stupid idiot she had been to think she could cheat him! She had given him information that he thought would lead him to Eric's plans, perhaps also to Eric. Of course she hadn't, but that was hardly the point. Either way, he wasn't going to let her go. He didn't need her to help him, not after she had served her purpose of locating Eric for him. And, Michael. . . . What of poor innocent Michael, locked up heaven only knew where?

All she had was that night. Tomorrow would be too late. Somehow she had to find out where Michael was and get out of her prison to rescue him.

She surveyed her surroundings. They were as bleak as the living room where she had talked with Jacques. A rickety bed covered with moldy blankets, a dresser with two of its drawers missing, an empty closet, its door hanging by one hinge—these were the only furnishings in the room.

The window overlooked the back of the house, and from her position she gauged the distance to the ground. The house was on a high foundation but the fall to the ground couldn't be more than eight or nine feet. It didn't sound like a lot, but from where she was, it might have been Mount Everest. Still, it was her only means of escape, and she couldn't afford the luxury of cowardice.

Pushing up with both hands, she strained to dislodge the window from its closed position. Obviously it had been stuck in place for several seasons.

She had barely succeeded in her task when a noise sounded beyond the door. Footsteps were approaching from the far end of the hall.

Quickly she pushed her weight down on the window to shut it, then moved to the bed, where she managed to sit just as the door to her room opened and the man in the park appeared once again.

He looked around the darkening room, his eyes skipping from corner to corner, as if he thought she'd have the unlikely opportunity to fill the room with accomplices. "Just checking," he said at last. "Take care of yourself, okay?" he added offhandedly, starting to back out of the room.

"Wait!" Jenny called, as the door was about to close.

The man stuck his head into the room, his hand still on the outside doorknob. "Yeah?"

"I'd like to use the washroom, please."

"Okay, I guess so. There's one down the hall, but don't

try anything original, eh? There's no way you're going to get out of here unless we let you go."

Jenny didn't argue. She allowed the man to guide her down the dark hall to the bathroom. Closing the door, she leaned her head against the cool tile wall, thankful that she had managed to get out of at least one room. But this was still a prison.

Voices came from the room next door. The tile covering the bathroom wall seemed to carry the sound as if in an echo chamber, magnifying the whispers of men on the other side of the thin partition. Jenny listened intently.

"The boy's too smart for his own good," she heard, and she couldn't fail to identify the speaker—Jacques Montand.

Then another man cut in, she wasn't sure who. Possibly the driver of the black car. "What are you going to do with him?" he said, his voice low and gravelly.

Jenny's blood ran cold as she heard Jacques's calm reply. "Dispose of him. We have no choice."

"He's a kid—"

"Shut up! Who makes the decisions?"

"Okay, okay. I'll go over to Church Road tomorrow and take care of it. Only I don't like it much. He's only a kid."

Church Road. That was in Paris. Jenny knew the street well because she passed it every day on the way to work. Its row houses all looked identical, like paper dolls cut from the same mold.

"The kids today have big eyes and big mouths. We can't afford to take any chances."

"Give me the number of the place again," said the man with the gravelly voice. "All those places look alike."

"Three-forty-five. Apartment A."

Eagerly Jenny memorized the number. If she could get

out, she could save Michael. Somehow she had to reach a telephone to call the police.

The man from the park banged his fist against the bathroom door, urging her to return to her cell at the back of the house. It would be all right, she told herself. Somehow she'd manage to jump from the window and make her escape. It would be easy, easy . . . she repeated mentally on the way back to the room.

It was almost impossible for her to hold back the smile she felt inside her. Soon Michael and she would both be free. Soon.

But her happiness was short-lived. She entered her room, but rather than leaving her at the door and locking it after her, the stocky man entered, as well, and pulled a small hammer from his jacket.

Crossing to the window, he reached into his pants pocket and brought out a handful of nails. With mounting horror, Jenny watched as he drove the nails into the windowsill, securely locking the window.

As he walked across the room, finished with his job, he smiled at her. "Too late, if you were planning anything," he said , and closed the door, locking it from the outside.

Jenny ran from the bed to the window, pushing with all her might to get it open. But, of course, her efforts were in vain. She looked down at the row of nails driven into the wooden sill.

Tears of frustration and helplessness welled up in her eyes. She *had* to get out of the room—she had to get to Michael before it was too late.

Like a caged animal, she paced back and forth from one end of the room to the other, moving now in circles, then backtracking and beginning over again in another direction. She could feel hysteria mounting from deep within her, and she knew that she would fall apart if she didn't make an effort to control herself.

She collapsed on the bed, emotionally beaten, physically drained. Her fingers moved restlessly over the cover beneath her body, working them into small gathers, like the folds of an oriental fan that when spread open would produce answers rather than purposeless designs.

Suddenly she stopped her aimless movements and stared at the material within her fingers. Then, in increasing excitement, she looked thoughtfully at the room.

It was a chance, only a chance, but one worth taking. Quietly, listening for sounds in the hallway beyond her room, she crept across the floor to the window. The panes of glass were thin, but then she hadn't thought they would be a problem. What had concerned her was the wood that supported each pane. Now, she could tell that her plan would work; the wood was thin and brittle.

She hurried back to the bed, stripping the blankets and what passed as sheets from the top and dragging everything back to the window. It was already dark outside and the moon was just beginning to rise, a pale mellow globe on the horizon.

That was unfortunate; the moonlight might expose her when she traveled across the field on her way to the road—if she got that far.

Picking up a strip of material from the floor, she bunched it over both her arms, creating a soft, protective shield that would take the impact of the glass as she forced herself against it, and at the same time muffle the sound of the breakage.

If she failed, then all was lost. Michael would be "disposed of" and she . . . . Jenny made a conscious effort not to think of Jacques Montand's rage when and if he caught her in her escape.

It had to be now.

Using all her strength, she heaved the full force of her upper body and arms against the window, shielding her face from the impact of glass shattering beneath the blow.

There was a crackling, splintering sound that to her ears sounded mightier than an explosion. She couldn't wait to see if anyone else had heard it. Moving her arms down to her waist, she quickly surveyed the result of her efforts.

The bottom panes had cracked away, leaving pieces of jagged glass in some squares, freeing others completely. But it was the wood that concerned her most. Some of it had broken apart and by tearing at it with her hands wrapped in sheets, she knew she'd be able to wedge enough of it away to make a hole large enough for her to squeeze through and out of the prison.

In less than five minutes, she had succeeded in her plan. She swallowed hard, and putting one knee up on the window ledge, gingerly she balanced herself precariously on the outside ledge while she prepared to jump.

Overhead the moon had passed behind a sheathing of clouds, causing the ground below to look dark, foreboding, a sea ready to swallow her.

She inched herself forward, hesitated, then dropped.

Her knees were raw and bleeding from the hard landing on sharp stones beneath the window. Otherwise she was intact. Like an animal scurrying for cover, she raced ahead to a clump of bushes near the house, pausing when she reached them to catch her breath and determine her next course.

From this new vantage point she saw not one, but two

automobiles parked in front of the house. The Citroën and
one other she had never seen before. They had been driven
to the house over a long driveway, which she assumed
turned off from a nearby main road. It was too dark to tell
for sure. If she cut across the field to her right, she'd be able
to avoid the driveway and still reach the road—providing
there was one.

She made a headlong dash for her goal, keeping her eyes
fixed on her destination. Only a little farther, a little far
ther; it would be over if she could manage just a short
distance more.

She had reached the road. Scrambling over a wooden
railed fence, she felt the joy of hard-packed dirt beneath
her feet. Behind her she could see the lights of the farm
house. No one had stirred. Yet.

The moon had emerged once again, its light her enemy,
shining on her form and creating shadows that appeared
and disappeared with her progress. She had turned right
onto the road, not knowing whether there was anything
close by in either direction. It was a purely random choice,
but an all-important one, for a boy's life depended on it be
ing correct.

Once more she ran, her heart pumping wildly now and
her lungs screaming as she pushed herself forward.
Dreamlike, she ran, her feet moving, but the scenery re
mained the same, inescapable nothingness of cow pastures,
empty fields and trees standing in clusters, silent spectators
to her deadly marathon.

Far beyond, a faint glow appeared on the horizon. She
pushed herself faster, the pain in her side now excruciating
and tears coming, forcing themselves from her eyes and
stinging her face in the rushing night air.

Driving onward without pausing, she twisted her head

to check behind her. The light still shone from the farmhouse window, the same light she had seen when scaling the fence; but now there was a second light, larger and more pronounced against the darkness.

Someone had opened the front door. Within its frame, shapes appeared, men silhouetted by a fringe of light. They were leaving the house to hunt her down and return her to her prison . . . and possibly to do worse, now that she had defied them.

Ahead, the glow on the horizon shone like a beacon and she plunged forward to its promise of safety.

A motor started in the distance behind her. She heard it stall. There was quiet again, then the sound of the engine being tried once more, this time catching, and being revved for the chase. She heard the car's terrible roar as it shot from the farmhouse down the narrow, pitted driveway and onto the street.

If only she could go on, if only she could go faster . . . .

The headlights behind her were getting close now; they sliced through the night like evil eyes, gleaming and hungry for her.

She stumbled from fatigue and picked herself up, summoning her last ounce of adrenalin to carry her forward to the light in front of her. It had become a blur in the distance. Nothing else mattered anymore; there was nothing around her, nothing in her consciousness but reaching that light.

The roar of an engine broke through her senses, jolting her back into the real world once more. The car was bearing down the road at full speed behind her.

Bushes and small shrubs dotted the side of the road in infrequent clumps. Some were near, but too low to provide refuge from the car's searching lights. The grass was low, too, perhaps six inches at the most. There was no place to hide.

The car was no more than a hundred yards behind her now. Desperate and exhausted, she flung herself into the grass at the side of the road, burying her face into the earth and flattening her body to its contours.

The car passed, leaving in its wake a high whine like a scream of vengeance.

She was safe.

Raising her head, she watched as the red taillights disappeared from her view. With any luck, the men would stop at the lighted place she'd been trying to reach, ask questions, and move on to continue their hunt farther down the road.

Then she'd be able to make it to the light herself and get help for Michael. Dragging herself back onto her feet, she trudged down the road again, her gait erratic as she exacted the last bit of strength from her legs wracked by muscle spasms.

Again the night was quiet, the countryside at peace; the moon tinted the landscape with a wash of silver mist.

Suddenly, unexpectedly, a sound shot through the air, ripping the silence apart. Jenny whirled around in horror. Two globes of bright, cold light bore down upon her; two headlights illuminated her on the road.

"No. . . ."

The car screeched to a halt and the passenger door sprang open.

Jacques Montand had no need to use force; his quarry was already broken.

Chapter 11

Jenny awoke, roused by the sharp voices in the next room. For a moment she was bewildered. Pushing herself up on her elbows, she looked around, still groggy from the effects of a sleep that had been all too short. She tried to remember why she was in this room with its peeling wallpaper of faded pink and yellow roses, and with a window that was partially covered by nailed slats of wood resembling bars. Then she remembered.

Her body ached from the previous night's exertion. But other than that she wasn't hurt although she could have been. Strangely enough, it had been Jacques who had restricted the man he called Gonzales from punishing her, as Gonzales had intended.

But today she might not be so fortunate. She had no doubt she had been spared last night's scene of retribution only because Jacques needed her today. If she were to enter a bank, she'd have to look presentable or risk unwanted attention.

Beyond the physical discomfort she felt, there was a

worse pain of knowing she had failed Michael. Jacques's cruel words still rang in her ears. "Dispose of him. We have no choice."

A new sound intruded upon her thoughts; somewhere a telephone was ringing. She had not expected that particular sound in these isolated surroundings, but she should have known that Jacques would see to every last detail that would aid him in his nefarious plans.

Sound passed easily through the thin walls; after all, that was why she had been placed in the room next to Jacques's point of operation. None of her movements would go undetected.

"You fool! You stupid idiot!"

Jenny could almost feel the rancor in Jacques's voice through the walls. He was screaming into the telephone. "You let him trick you again. I never left here, do you understand? I couldn't have given you those orders." There was a pause on Jacques's end of the conversation as the person on the other end of the phone spoke. Then he shouted, "What about the kid? At least you've got him, haven't you?"

Jenny bolted upright in bed, her heart beating a wild racing tattoo within her chest. *Michael.*

"Stupid!" Jacques burst forth with a tirade of invectives, hurled nonstop at the caller. Jenny almost felt sorry for him. "If you keep this up, you'll go back to picking pockets on the Via Veneto. I was a fool to let you join us in the first place. You're nothing but a petty street thief. Get over here, and hurry!"

The phone was slammed down, the impact reverberating in Jenny's ears. *Michael was gone!* Somehow Michael had escaped! No. Not just somehow. Unless she was completely mistaken, the man who had freed her brother had to have been Eric.

She heard footsteps in the hall outside her room. They stopped as their owner paused outside her door and twisted a key in the lock. Swinging open with force, the door slammed against the wall and bounced back, almost hitting Jacques as he stood framed in the doorway, his face dark with barely suppressed anger. Kicking the door shut with his heel, he remained just within the room, not more than three steps from the door. Contemplatively he flipped the key in the air, catching it and sending it forth again.

"Stand," he ordered.

Jenny obeyed, slowly moving her legs off the bed and onto the wooden floor. Thin scabs had formed over the knees, beginning the healing process that would repair the flesh, torn in last night's aborted escape.

Montand's eyes traveled over her. Jenny backed away, afraid of what his glance conveyed. But she was wrong.

"You're a mess," he said at last. "You can't go anywhere like that."

He was right. Her clothes had been torn beyond repair. Deep green grass stains, like sickly gashes splotched over the material of her once white blouse. Her shoes lay nearby on the floor, small nails protruding from one of them where the heel had once been.

There was no way she could play the respectable customer making a routine withdrawal from her safety deposit box.

"What's your size? I'll send someone to get things for you to wear." He wrote down the information she gave him on a small note pad.

It was like being dressed for a funeral. She was a goose being trussed for Christmas dinner. He would clothe her in attractive goods and she would lead him to a location that would eventually mean her demise. Unless, of course, she could get away. Obviously though, she would be watched much more closely now. After all, she had given them quite a run.

"You heard?" he asked, seemingly aware of the sound of a man walking in the next room.

Naturally he'd know she would have been able to hear his telephone conversation. "Yes. I assume from what I heard that Michael is gone. He's free." she replied, unable to keep a note of triumph out of her voice.

"Michael is free; but not you."

Jenny studied her captor's face, the same handsome face of a man she loved. Only now she realized that except for the superficial resemblance, there was very little the two men held in common—apart, of course, from their criminal involvements.

Like Eric, Jacques could be charming, but beneath the polished veneer ran a streak of cruelty so apparent to her now she wondered how she could ever have missed it. It was difficult to believe a man like Jacques Montand could move among decent people and go undetected for what he was—a ruthless, driving criminal. Restraints of decency that impeded others from performing criminal acts meant nothing to him. And nothing and no one obstructed him from carrying out his unscrupulous activities. No one, perhaps, except one man—Eric Delmont, Jacques's nemesis extraordinaire.

"Could you actually have . . . disposed . . . of Michael? A child?" she asked; finding herself morbidly curious.

He met her gaze boldly. "If it was necessary."

"And it was," she said, as a matter of fact.

Jacques smiled back at her coldly and without shame.

A sharp feeling of uneasiness passed over her. "And when you're through with me?"

"Then we will have to see." His eyes narrowed as he

studied her. "Indeed, Jennifer Gordon, you are a most beautiful creature." He drew the words out lovingly, then changed to the clipped meter of technical analysis. "It would be a pity to find no suitable use for you. But, alas, my dear, you've made yourself extremely unreliable in my estimation. The stunt last night was most unfortunate. It did nothing to help insure your future."

"My life, you mean."

"If you wish, then," he nodded deferentially. "Your life."

Oh, yes, it was all quite clear. The only thing she had to bargain with was the story about the papers Eric maintained in the bank. He must still believe her, or he certainly wouldn't trouble himself with getting clothes for her appearance in public.

But her stay of execution would be a short-lived reprieve at best. Once she stepped from the bank vault empty-handed, she'd be able to measure the remaining moments of her life in minutes.

Jacques had finished with her. He opened the door to her room and exited, leaving her locked and alone to contemplate the very real horror of his last words.

Lifeless roses of pale pink and yellow surrounded her like someone's hideous joke of a bizarre funeral wreath, the dislodged strips of wallpaper waving in an unseen breeze like mourners at an elaborate death procession.

She had heard accounts related by people who had been close to death—as she most certainly must be—and how those people had seen their lives pass before them in a clear, quick instant. But such was not to be her case.

She had no time to dwell in the past; the present was too urgent. Somehow she'd fight Jacques Montand to the end—however near it may be. But how?

The new clothes were brought to her two hours later. The dress selected was in gray, no doubt a good choice by Jacques's standards, as it would do little to attract attention, blending into the serene atmosphere of the bank. Shoes, also in gray, had been purchased, and to Jenny's amazement they fit surprisingly well. A wash basin of water had been provided, along with a towel and some soap.

Fifteen minutes after she had been presented with her new wardrobe, Jacques reappeared at her door.

"Good, you're dressed. Let me see you." He appraised her appearance with a professional sweep of his eyes. "You'll do fine. Come, there's breakfast waiting in the other room. I can't have you fainting on me when we're in Paris."

How typical, Jenny thought, disgusted. Everything planned to the last detail, orchestrated around his desires and schemes. Were it not inconvenient for him, she knew he wouldn't care if she starved to death.

She followed him from the room into the hall beyond. He pushed her inside the room next to hers, the one with the telephone.

Breakfast was still warm. Eggs, apparently brought in from some nearby restaurant, were still warm and a box containing muffins was placed in the center of the table, along with a carafe of steaming coffee.

He motioned for her to sit.

"Eat," he barked.

It was an order not to be refused and obediently she lifted her fork. But the lack of food over the past day had diminished her appetite rather than stimulated it. She picked at the eggs, feeling, as Jacques had predicted, suddenly faint.

Sitting across the table, he poured himself some coffee and sipped it slowly, watching her over the rim of the cup.

With a sudden movement, he slammed the cup down on the table, spraying the scalding liquid over his arm. Enraged, he rose with such force that his chair skidded behind him and toppled on its side.

Jenny dropped her fork, frightened by the outburst. He walked around the table and grabbed her shoulders, shaking her as he bellowed in uncontrollable rage.

"I told you to eat! Enough has gone wrong already; you're not going to spoil anything else, do you hear? Do you understand? Now eat!"

She trembled and reached for the fork, but her compliance to his demand was not fast enough to please him. Impatient, he grabbed the fork from her hand and began stabbing at the eggs himself, losing control as he brought the utensil to her mouth, causing the eggs to spill back to the plate.

Furious now, he pulled her from the chair, shaking her like a rag doll as he vented his suppressed anger and frustration.

But for Jenny the last two days had taken their toll. She felt herself spinning . . . then it was the room that spun, in crazy tilted spirals. She tried to steady herself, reaching out to the empty space around her, but her legs began to buckle. As she teetered at the edge of blackness, she was stunned into reality by the sharp impact of Jacques's hand striking her across the face. The blow sent her reeling backward against the wall and he moved toward her, his arm raised high above her.

Cringing, she moved sideways to avoid the assault. His breathing was loud and heavy, coming in short gasps as he lunged for her again.

A shock wave exploded through the room. The sound of splintering wood preceded an explosion of footsteps, then a man's deep voice rang out.

"Halt!"

Jacques Montand spun on his heels, his face white and startled as he stared at the kitchen door that had been kicked open, and also at the man dressed in ordinary street clothes who was crouched down on one knee, leveling an automatic revolver in firing position.

"Get your hands up," the man commanded.

Jacques made a sudden move, a reflex action of flight, but stopped just in time to prevent the man from firing.

Jenny was backed against the wall, flattening herself to it in wide-eyed fear as she watched the scene unfold before her.

Two more men appeared at the door; policemen wearing uniforms. A third uniformed man soon joined them.

"Over there," the man holding the gun barked at Jacques, pointing several feet to the side of where he was now standing.

Jacques obeyed, moving slowly to the side, his eyes darting nervously from the gun in the man's hand to the three policemen standing just within the doorway.

"Turn around and keep your hands raised."

A police officer frisked Jacques, throwing a switchblade and a small revolver behind him for one of his compatriots to retrieve and hold as evidence.

"Are you all right, Miss Gordon?" the first man, still holding the gun, inquired.

"I'm fine . . . I think," she replied weakly, then realized she had been called by her name. Puzzled, she watched as the two policemen at the door drew apart, allowing yet another man to enter the room.

Jenny gasped in astonished disbelief. It was Eric Delmont!

"Mr. Delmont, we've got your man. Care to make the official identification?"

Eric moved slowly into the center of the room, his eyes not on Jacques Montand, but on Jenny.

"Mr. Delmont?" the officer prodded.

"Yes," Eric responded, turning his attention to Jacques, who glared at him with unconcealed hatred from across the room.

Eric walked closer to the thief, his eyes steady, probing the face of the master criminal.

"So, Mr. Delmont, we finally meet," said Jacques coldly.

"You should have realized that our introduction, such as it is, would be inevitable. You became too greedy, Montand. Too bold."

"I was very good at my job. It could have gone on indefinitely, were it not for your meddling, Delmont."

Eric seemed to consider the statement. "Perhaps you're right. But as good as you were, you must admit—I was even better. As proof . . . I offer the present situation," he said, smiling grimly.

"Who are you, Delmont?" Jacques looked at the police. "You aren't one of them, are you?" he sneered. "It would be a terrible waste of talent."

"Who I am is none of your concern, but, no, I'm not with the police. I'm also not a thief." He looked up and stared directly at Jenny.

The officer in plain clothes moved next to Eric. "We'll be taking him in now. This time he's going to be out of commission for a good, long time. Thanks to you, sir," he added.

"I presume you've already taken care of the accomplices?" Eric questioned.

"Yes, that's all been handled," the man replied.

"We'll take the lady home, too," one of the officers volunteered, crossing to Jenny.

"Thank you, but that won't be necessary, officer. I've already made plans for the lady."

Jenny met Eric's glance. She didn't know what she felt; her confusion at the moment was total.

Eric was not with the police, and apparently he was not a criminal, either. She had judged him wrongly on that count. Also to his credit, according to Monica, he had called her at the travel agency.

Yet there was still the episode with Candy in Copenhagen to consider. No matter what he had professed to feel for her, he obviously found Candy McManus equally absorbing of his emotions.

For once she would be wise and do the sensible thing. Eric—whoever he really was, and whatever he really did—had devastated her emotionally. She couldn't bear to experience that kind of pain again. They were both safe, and her suspicions about him had been nullified. Better to leave things as they were.

"I appreciate the offer, Mr. Delmont," she said stiffly, "but I think it might be wiser for me to take advantage of the officer's kind offer."

Eric gave a sigh. "No, Miss Gordon, you will not take the officer's kind offer. You will take *my* kind offer."

With that he took her arm, and led her gently out of the room, down the hall to the porch beyond and down the several steps to the driveway.

A black Mercedes sports car was parked at the edge of the driveway near the police vehicles. Politely he opened the door and waited for her to slide into the seat. When she didn't, he turned her around to face him.

"Leave me alone, Eric," she pleaded.

His eyes searched her face. "You don't mean that, and you know it as well as I do."

"Well, you're wrong. I've had enough. I still don't know who you are. I don't know what you do. And I don't know what you feel. There are too many unanswered questions for me, Eric."

She drew away from him, backing off slowly as if allowing herself time to memorize his face; then abruptly she turned and ran back to the house.

"You're a stubborn woman, Jennifer Gordon!" he called after her. "But it won't do you any good—I'm stubborn, too!"

Chapter 12

Monica rushed from the front door of Jenny's house, just as the police officer dropped her off.

"Jenny! You're safe. Oh, Jenny. . . ." with that, she threw her arms around Jenny, hugging her close. "Michael's home," she said, drawing away and helping Jenny walk to the house. "You look exhausted."

Jenny finally learned some of the details. Monica had called the police when Jenny hadn't returned home. She'd told them the story of Michael's abduction, and of how Eric Delmont was in some way involved. It was all she could tell them, and it wasn't much, but apparently, it had been enough. The man who'd been holding Michael captive was a petty crook who made many mistakes, leaving a trail that led to Michael's discovery. After Eric had secured the young lad's release by impersonating Jacques, he and the police had simply followed the man to the farmhouse when he had driven to meet Montand.

"It's all over now," Jenny said listlessly. "It's all over." And the second statement referred to her relationship with Eric.

"YOU'RE LOOKING GOOD, kid," Anne said, several days later as they lunched at their favorite café. "But sad."

"I'm fine," Jenny protested.

"No, you're not. Put that sandwich down and look at me, Jen."

Jenny knew better than to argue. It was easier just to let Anne get whatever she had to say out of her system.

"This is how it is, friend. Your outside bruises have healed nicely. There's that same gorgeous face—good as new. But inside you're miserable. Call him."

"I don't know his number," Jenny said, knowing it would be futile to pretend she didn't know who Anne meant.

"That's no problem. Quentin has many sources—you want information? You've got it."

"No!" Jenny said, more loudly than necessary.

"Why then are you still wearing that necklace if you don't care about him? Answer me that."

"I like it. It . . . it just seems right somehow that I should keep it."

Anne nodded wisely. "Okay, have it your way."

Jenny looked at her friend suspiciously. Anne had never given up so easily before.

ANNE AND QUENTIN HAD INSISTED she be ready to leave at ten o'clock on Saturday morning. For her friend's sake Jenny had agreed to go. There was to be an enormous party held at one of Quentin's friends' country estates and Anne was terrified of going alone, without an old friend along.

"I'll probably use the wrong fork or something, and make a complete fool of myself," she had said, coaxing her to say yes. "Quentin has to mingle; he can't hold my hand the whole time."

"Remember what happened the last time you dragged

me off to one of your galas," Jenny cautioned. "My life hasn't been the same since."

"I know, I know. But this is different, I promise."

So Jenny was ready. Anne had insisted on checking out every last piece of clothing Jenny planned to wear. "Wear something gorgeous . . . smashing," she had begged. "I want you to look stunning and show all those snobs with money what *real* class is."

She had also been adamant that Jenny wear the pendant Eric had given her.

The estate they visited was unlike any Jenny had seen before. Multilevels of the stone house cantilevered over a man-made stream, its watery bed cast in concrete, running from story to story around the estate's perimeter.

It was a masterpiece of modern architecture, and in spite of its clean lines, it was every bit as impressive as Château des Fleurs had been with its ancient turrets and gargoyles. The home seemed to blend into the wooded terrain surrounding it, making it a part of nature rather than an unwelcome intrusion.

A waterfall cascaded from an upper level to a reflecting pool near the entrance, creating a musical symphony that only nature could produce as sweetly.

"What do you think?" Anne asked, nudging Jenny with her elbow.

"I think you've got sharp elbows," said Jenny, grimacing. But she had to admit she was more than a little impressed.

A butler answered the door and led them into a huge open room flooded by natural light from skylights overhead. The room's appointments were in soft shades of cream that took on tones of light yellow and peach depending upon the time of day. It was a soft and arresting interior, made even more comfortable by the use of live trees growing in enormous white ceramic containers. Here and there a piece of sculpture had been placed on a pedestal, and paintings Jenny easily identified as the work of Dali or Chagall graced the huge expanses of white walls.

People were sitting on low, built-in couches and chairs, talking quietly among themselves, while soft classical music floated above their voices from an unseen speaker system.

Jenny was completely entranced. She could easily spend the rest of her life among such surroundings. *But, then, who couldn't*, she thought, as she drew apart from Quentin and Anne who had joined a small circle of people near the entrance.

A wide stairway covered in the same plush cream carpeting, led to a higher level that Jenny longed to explore for more intriguing artwork. Submitting to her desire, she found herself in a long gallery. The walls of three of its sides were lined with paintings, while the remaining wall, a solid sheet of plate glass, provided a view of the fields surrounding the estate.

The terrain had been kept natural, and in the far distance, as she looked from the window, she could see a family of deer moving through tall grass.

Absorbed in her thoughts, she didn't hear the footsteps that fell quietly on the carpet behind her until it was too late.

There was a sudden pull at her neck and she felt the weight of the pendant slip away. Her hand shot up, clutching at nothing but bare skin where the necklace had been only a second before. It was history repeating itself; another party—another theft. And she couldn't stand it.

She felt sick and immobilized with fear. The scream that

welled up from deep within her she stifled, realizing that it would serve only to anger the thief. No one would hear her cry in this isolated part of the vast house.

She shuddered, recoiling as a cold hand touched her arm and a voice broke into the silence.

"I told you that I was stubborn."

Jenny reeled around to face the man who had spoken. "Eric!" she gasped. "What are you doing here?" Looking down, she saw the pendant in his hands.

"I'm giving a party for some of my friends," he replied innocently.

"You own all of this?" she asked in wonder. Her eyes traveled over the wall of paintings. Then they clouded. She started away, calling over her shoulder as she walked, "So you've tricked me into coming here. This was all planned, wasn't it?"

Eric moved quickly, stopping her with his hand.

"Yes," he admitted. "It was all planned, but isn't that what you wanted? You said you didn't know anything about me, and you wouldn't allow me to explain, so what better way is there than to show you?"

"You tricked me," repeated Jenny, shaking her head. "You and Anne."

"She cares for you very much, believe me," said Eric softly. "I'll admit that we tricked you. But you wouldn't have come if we hadn't, would you?"

"No, because it would have been pointless. And still is."

With that, she turned on her heel and once again started to walk away. Once again, she was stopped by Eric's restraining hand.

"Wait!" he pleaded, and there was something in his voice that held her back; a note almost of desperation. Surprised, she turned hesitantly toward him, searching his face for an answer to her unspoken question.

"I can understand why you're afraid of becoming involved with me. But you're wrong, Jenny," he said quietly. "At least let me explain. Don't throw away the most precious possession that either of us could ever own."

Jenny followed his eyes as they moved around the room, resting on individual paintings of priceless worth.

"Don't you see," he added gently, "none of this means anything to me without you."

Reluctantly Jenny listened, and over the next few minutes learned the answers to so many of the questions that had plagued her over the past months.

Far from being the thief she'd originally thought, Eric was the son of the chairman of the board of Global Insurance Corporation, a giant multinational firm headquartered in London. When several of their most prestigious clients were robbed of their jewels, their own investigators, assisted by the police, tracked down a prime suspect—one Jacques Montand.

Eric had become involved in the case for one reason only—his uncanny resemblance to Jacques. Unable to flush Montand out, one of the cleverest operators they had ever encountered, Interpol had enlisted Eric to aid them.

The plan was to cause Montand so much trouble and aggravation, that eventually he would seek Eric, thus exposing himself to the police. "And it worked," he finished with a grin, "thanks to you."

"What about Copenhagen?" asked Jenny, still skeptical. Slowly but surely she could feel her hesitancy, her unwillingness to believe him, melting away, but she'd been through too much to be easily convinced.

Eric gave her a wry smile. "That," he replied sincerely, "was one of the worst moments of my life. Candy McManus was a plant. She was working with me to lure Montand out of his lair, so to speak. We had gone to a lot of trouble to set that evening up. The publicity in the newspapers and on television had advertised Candy's plans—and her wealth. If Montand was any kind of a thief, he'd make an appearance to grab her jewels. I didn't dare risk your safety by speaking to you. Nor could I abandon my plans and take you off somewhere to explain the situation because time was too critical and too many people had worked so hard to set up the ruse."

"And you couldn't explain later, because you didn't know where I worked or lived," murmured Jenny, almost to herself, as she remembered Monica's duplicity.

Eric's only reply was a look of reproach. "What about Marrakesh?" asked Jenny suddenly.

For a moment, Eric's face was blank. "What about it?" he queried.

"It wasn't you I saw at dinner that night? With an older woman."

Eric shook his head in firm denial, "No, it must have been Jacques you saw. I admit, I was in Marrakesh, but I had no idea you were there, too."

Jenny nodded slowly as her last reserves melted away. Only one thought prevented her from capitulating completely. "And Candy?" She asked anxiously. "Who is she exactly? Is she really a friend of your family—or just a policewoman?"

Eric laughed. "Candy is the daughter of one of my father's long-time friends. More importantly, she is rich . . . that's why we used her. Montand was too clever to fall for a phony setup. He'd have sources to check out whether she was legitimate, and more important, that her jewels were real."

"And she doesn't . . . mean anything to you?"

"She's nothing more than a good, and very brave, friend," replied Eric emphatically.

Jenny smiled slightly. "I guess the timing was pretty bad when we met that night at the Château des Fleurs."

He nodded. "It couldn't have been worse. In fact, if I hadn't have been so involved with you, I would probably have been able to stop Montand that evening. You can't imagine how rotten I felt having to leave you there, and then at the restaurant, as well. It almost killed me, Jenny," he said seriously, looking at her with tender concern. "But I didn't dare involve you. There was always the terrifying possibility that you could have been hurt—seriously."

"I almost was," she replied, thinking about her experience with Jacques in the farmhouse. "I'm glad you told me all this. At last."

"There's an enormous crowd of people downstairs," Eric said, taking her hands in his, "but to tell you the truth, I'm slightly embarrassed about this party."

"Embarrassed? But, why?"

"It's a little awkward for me today, because it's been a tradition with me that I always throw parties with central themes."

"Like a hunting theme? A May Day theme? Something like that, you mean?"

"Exactly. Everyone's just come to expect it." He shook his head, as if at a loss. "But today . . . well, I had something planned, but I'm not sure it's entirely appropriate."

"What is it?"

"You'll be honest if I tell you?"

"Absolutely. I promise," Jenny said, holding her hand up as if taking an oath.

Eric reached into his pocket and withdrew a matchbox in black velvet with beautiful gold scrollwork etched on its cover. It reminded Jenny of the book of matches he had given her the night at Chez Cary.

"I'd almost forgotten," Eric said, staring at the matchbox in his hand. "You have a penchant for matches, don't you? Here," he said, handing the box to her.

Jenny studied the elaborate gold calligraphy on its cover, a JG intertwined with an ED. Their initials.

Puzzled, she looked up. "Open it," he urged.

She pushed the miniature drawer at one end, sliding it out to expose a small parcel wrapped in gold silk. Again she looked up, and Eric coaxed her with his eyes to continue.

The silk fell away from her fingers and in her hand she held a magnificent ring with a diamond solitaire. Jenny stared at it in bewilderment.

"It's fabulous," she gasped. "The color is incredible."

Against the light from the window, the stone burst forth with the brilliance of fire as it caught the slightest color in the surroundings and reflected it back tenfold. "Why, it must be three carats at least," she said, turning it around in her hand.

"Five," Eric corrected. "And it's a perfect stone. It's been in my family for generations."

"Like the pendant," she murmured feeling somehow lost without it hanging around her neck.

"Exactly. Like the pendant."

"It's truly magnificent, Eric," she said, handing it back. "Thank you for letting me see it."

"It's yours."

"But—"

"No protests," he interrupted firmly. "A bargain is a bargain. I told you the night at the Chez Cary that you'd have to wear the pendant until I replaced it with something else. Well, this is it. Only there's one problem." A dark look crossed his face, alarming her. He put his hand on her arm, cautioning her. "It's got to stay in the family."

Jenny wrinkled her brow, understanding, yet not entirely sure she had heard correctly.

"I'm asking you to marry me, Jenny," he said softly.

"Eric—"

He held up his hand, silencing her protest before she had a chance to voice it. "All right, you don't have to answer that question now. But you already gave me your word that you'd tell me if you thought my idea for a theme for the party would be suitable."

"Yes," she admitted. "I did."

"Very well," he continued, taking her arm and guiding her along the gallery in the direction of the door. "You see, this was my plan. . . ." He lowered his voice to a confidential level: "I've had the chef prepare an enormous cake, very elaborate. Napkins have been printed up, and you know the matchbox you just saw? Well, I've had white ones like it made for all the guests. Oh . . . there's too much to explain. You'll just have to come down and see for yourself. In fact, they've been in works since last Christmas but, to tell you the truth, I was afraid I'd have to scrap the whole thing. I was delighted when Anne and Quentin came to me a week or so ago, because this was one bash I really wanted to hold. After all, it's not every day I throw an engagement party."

Jenny stopped and turned to face him, her eyes filling with tears.

"No?" Eric's face fell. "Then you don't think it's a good theme?"

"No," she said, a tear falling down her cheek, "I don't think it's a good theme." She paused for added effect, then cried, "I think it's a wonderful theme! I think it's the most wonderful idea I've ever heard!" Throwing her arms around his neck, she allowed him to lift her and spin her in circles.

"There's only one thing, Eric," she said, as they walked down the stairs to the large room filled with waiting guests. "It's about your artwork."

Eric looked down, concern written on his face. "You don't care for it?"

"Well," she said, "I'll admit you have a few very nice pieces, but we're going to have to get rid of some of them."

"Of course. If there are artists you prefer . . . ."

"Yes," she whispered, as if the spirits of the modern masters were lurking nearby. "There's a very fine artist I know of—not well-known yet—but you'll be able to get a terrific deal on the paintings."

"Fine, whatever you want. What's the chap's name, anyway? If you really like him that much, we'll buy up everything he's done"

"The artist is a woman," said Jenny. "And it won't be necessary to spend a penny. I've got all of them myself already. They're in my closet at home. About fifty original Jennifer Gordons, I believe."

Eric smiled, "Ah, yes, I've heard of the artist. Only I believe her name is being changed soon. To Delmont."

"Forever," Jenny whispered, and held tightly to his hand as they entered the room with waiting guests.

MYSTIQUE BOOKS

Experience the warmth of love... and the threat of danger!

MYSTIQUE BOOKS are a breathless blend of romance and suspense, passion and mystery. Let them take you on journeys to exotic lands—the sunny Caribbean, the enchantment of Paris, the sinister streets of Istanbul.

MYSTIQUE BOOKS

An unforgettable reading experience.
Now...many previously published titles are once again available.
Choose from this great selection!

Don't miss any of these thrilling novels of love and adventure!

Choose from this list of exciting
MYSTIQUE BOOKS